THE
WHODUNNIT
MURDER

THE WHODUNNIT MURDER

Roger Keevil

a Ramston murder mystery

also by Roger Keevil

**THE INSPECTOR CONSTABLE MURDER
MYSTERIES**
Murderer's Fête
Murder Unearthed
Death Sails In The Sunset
Murder Comes To Call
Murder Most Frequent
The Odds On Murder
No Bar To Murder
The Murder Cabinet
The Game Of Murder

THE COPPER & CO MURDER MYSTERIES
Honeymooner's Murder
Murder At Witch's Holt
Buccaneer's Murder

THE RAMSTON MURDER MYSTERIES
Murdered By Moonlight
Manuscript For Murder

THE WHODUNNIT MURDER

by

Roger Keevil

Cover design by Christopher Brooke

Copyright © 2023 Roger Keevil

The moral right of the author has been asserted.

'The Whodunnit Murder' is a work of fiction and wholly the product of the imagination of the author. All persons, events, locations, organisations and establishments are entirely fictitious or are used fictitiously, and are not intended to resemble in any way any actual persons living or dead, events, locations, organisations, or establishments. Any such resemblance is entirely coincidental, and is wholly in the mind of the reader.

This book is dedicated to all real authors
who do not believe that A.I. is the future.

Chapter 1

"Murder?"

"Yes!" came the enthusiastic response.

"Really?" Tania Faye quirked a sceptical eyebrow.

"Yes. Why not? It'd be fun," insisted the other.

"Jenny." Tania, Head Librarian at the Central Library in the heart of the market town of Ramston, took a deep breath and let out a long patient sigh. "Do you honestly think that, in the aftermath of the murders I've been caught up in recently, I can regard the topic under the heading of 'fun'?"

"No, but this is different." Jenny Chandler, the dental nurse who worked as Tania's part-time Saturday library assistant, glowed with enthusiasm. "One of the girls at the practice was talking about it the other day. She and her boyfriend went to one of these whodunnit evenings they have at the Ramston Chase Hotel, and they had a great time. And it's not serious at all, honestly. No real blood or anything. Emily said it was all a good laugh. I just thought something like that might take your mind off having had to deal with the real thing." The young woman seemed downcast at Tania's cool reception to what she obviously thought was something of a brainwave.

Tania took pity on her assistant. "All right then." She surveyed the practically deserted library. "As we're quiet at the moment, you'd better tell me what it's all about."

Jenny settled her generous frame into a chair alongside Tania's desk and lowered her voice to a conspiratorial level. "Like I said, Emily explained it all to me at work. It starts off with someone being

7

killed ..."

"I hope this wasn't while you were in the midst of treating a patient," smiled Tania. "I can't imaging being seated in the dentist's chair while tales of gruesome murder are being exchanged across my helpless body. Thoughts of Sweeney Todd spring to mind."

"No, it was during our coffee break," laughed Jenny. "Alison would have had my skin if I'd said anything like that in front of a patient."

"Thank goodness. So, back to the beginning. Who does this killing? Is it the hotel, or what?"

"No," explained Jenny. "There's a firm that does it all. Emily said they're called 'Murder At Your Place', or something like that. There's two chaps who arrange everything, and they play the detectives. It all happens during dinner, and they choose some people at the start to be the suspects. Emily got to be one, but she didn't actually have to do anything except read out a couple of statements on cards during the evening. Clues and things, she said. And then the detective starts by saying there's been a murder, but you don't actually get to see that, which I think is a bit of a swizz, and he says that he wants everyone to help work out who did it from the clues. And they get revealed all through the evening, during the meal."

"It doesn't sound all that exciting," demurred Tania. "You might as well get fish and chips and play a murder board game at home."

"Oh no," said Jenny. "Because here's the fun bit. Emily says that every so often, in between courses, the inspector says he's going to send his sergeant off to look for a 'witness', and the other chap comes back a few minutes later dressed up as somebody else. In this one, first of all it was a schoolboy in

8

short trousers, and then after that it was a mad old vicar, and they got interviewed to reveal some clues." Jenny let out a giggle. "And according to Emily, the vicar was wearing the most horrible false teeth, and he was spraying his words all over the place."

"Sounds delightful. Even so ..."

"Oh no, there's more," gurgled Jenny. "The best bit was the last witness, because when the sergeant chap came back, he was dressed as a woman! Wig, high heels, the lot, and a huge chest! And this was meant to be the Lady Mayoress of the town. Emily said she was in fits. Well, everyone was."

"I can imagine."

"So at the end of the meal, everyone had to fill in a card saying who they thought did it, and what the evidence was, and the inspector gave the solution."

"The classic Poirot scene," remarked Tania. "And that was it?"

"Oh no. They did a bit where the guilty suspect got handcuffed and taken away – well, not really – and then they handed out the prizes."

"There are prizes? That sounds rather more like it."

"Yes. And Emily's boyfriend won! He worked everything out the best of everyone, and he got a certificate and a bottle of champagne!"

"Hmmm," murmured Tania. "More than I ever got from Inspector Copper. But I'm still not convinced that it's the sort of thing that Ron and I would enjoy."

"Well, I'm sure some people would," insisted Jenny, determined not to be put off. "In fact, I'm going to go along with Emily to the next one they put on at the hotel and try my luck. I could fancy winning a bottle of champagne."

"Knowing your luck, the best you're likely to get is a bottle of shampoo!" laughed Tania.

"Anyway," continued Jenny, delving into her handbag, "Emily picked up one of the flyers at the do. I thought I might pin it up on the library noticeboard in case anyone's interested. That's if it's okay with you."

"Go ahead," replied Tania. "We may as well see if there's anyone else in this town with as ghoulish a taste for murder as you."

"Bet you I'm right," retorted Jenny, jumping to her feet and heading for the board at the library's entrance where public notices were displayed.

*

"You'll never guess who I've been talking to," gushed Jenny as she arrived for work the following Saturday.

"In that case, since I don't have my detective head on at the moment, you'd better tell me," smiled Tania.

"My friend Alex."

"And your friend Alex is ...?" enquired Tania, none the wiser.

"We go to Zumba together on a Friday night," explained Jenny.

"You go to Zumba?" queried Tania, an eyebrow raised.

"Yes, I do, actually," said Jenny, slightly huffily. "And your point is ...?"

"Nothing, nothing at all," responded Tania hastily. "I ... I didn't know they did Zumba classes locally, that's all. Anyway, your friend Alex ...? He? She?"

Jenny giggled. "You don't get that many guys at Zumba! No, Alex is Alexandra. Alexandra Blaine. She's a researcher on 'Spotlight Today' at the TV studios."

"I still don't ..."

"And ... she's secretary of the Ramston Literary Society!" announced Jenny triumphantly.

"Oh, them." Tania's tone hinted at a degree of reservation. "Well, I've heard of them, of course, but I don't really know much about them. I know they book a meeting room at the Leisure Centre once in a while. As far as I'm aware, it's a rather grand name for a cross between a book-reading circle and a bunch of wannabe authors who can't actually get a publisher. At least, that's what Rudolph Wheatley once described them as."

"That stuck-up historian chap who got caught up in the murder at the abbey?" observed Jenny. "And what does he know?"

"He's a very well-respected author," replied Tania severely. "Although I must admit, he is a little grand."

"Too grand for the likes of Alex and her friends. She says they're just interested in reading for the fun of it, and some of them are trying to get stuff they've written out there so that people can read their work. I told Emily what Alex had said, and she said she'd always fancied trying to write a novel. You know – 'Scandal At The Dentist's', or something like that. So she's only gone and joined the Society, hasn't she, to see if they can help her do it? And they've made her Secretary. I told her, don't you let Alison catch you giving away people's secrets. But I think she's very brave. I couldn't ever write a book. So I don't think people should sneer."

"You're right," said Tania, contrite. "So, what was it that your friend Alex had to say?"

"She'd seen a notice that I put up at the health centre about the murder evenings, and she thought

11

it sounded fun, so she passed it on to the rest of the committee, and they agreed. And they've been in touch with the organisers to find out when the next do at the hotel is, and apparently they'll come and set things up at your own venue whenever you want. Isn't that great?"

"That's very nice for them, I'm sure," shrugged Tania. "But I still don't see why you're so excited at the prospect."

"Because," said Jenny, "they want to do it in the old reading room."

*

The Market Square at the centre of Ramston presented a pleasing confection of architectural styles. To one side, and dominating the townscape, rose the imposing mediaeval stone bulk of Ramston Abbey, still the heart and *raison d'être* of the town, despite its diminution at the time of Henry VIII's dissolution of the monasteries, becoming instead the town's parish church. But the abbey's down-grading meant new opportunities for the town. What had been the abbey's Great Court became the town's cobbled Market Square, now surrounded on all sides by a charming mixture of buildings, ranging from timber-framed Tudor merchants' houses which had miraculously survived the attentions of 'improvers' of later centuries, their ground floors hosting smart boutiques and craft shops, to elegant Georgian town-houses now occupied by law firms and insurance companies. Directly opposite the abbey stood a fine ancient stone structure, once the gatehouse to the religious precincts, then a coaching inn, now the Cross Keys Hotel, the town's favourite pub and restaurant. And along from the Cross Keys, the Town Hall.

In the eighteenth century, the leading citizens of Ramston had deemed the slightly ramshackle re-purposed former barn, one of the few surviving remnants of the abbey buildings which had served as the Town Hall, not suitable for the town's growing status, and had erected a modest porticoed structure in classical style in its place opposite the abbey. But when this burnt down in the nineteenth century, the town's burghers had grander ideas. There arose, in the latest high Victorian gothic style and built of the same stone as the abbey, a grandiose edifice of turrets, battlements, and oriel windows, a Town Hall to rival the most ambitious creations of England's northern industrial cities, albeit on a smaller scale. On the upper floor, to house the great and the good, a lofty panelled council chamber, with a mayor's parlour decorated in sumptuous Arthurian frescoes. And on the ground floor, so as not to neglect the authorities' duty to improve the lower classes, a generously-proportioned library and reading room.

And for over a century, those generous proportions proved perfectly adequate, but there came a time when the library outgrew its home. Then, in the 1960s, one of the council's architects devised a surprisingly empathetic solution. Adjacent to the library was a courtyard, originally used for the council's horse-drawn vehicles and their animals. With a touch of inspiration, the courtyard was roofed over to become a modern spacious library, while the old arched gateway became the Central Library's new entrance. And the old library became the town's new art gallery and exhibition space, a home for Ramston's justifiably-celebrated collection of historical and modern works of art, with an alcove at the end devoted to travelling displays from contemporary artists. The current installation, widely derided, by a well-known modern artist who was dismissively described by the local paper's arts correspondent as resembling one of her own unmade beds, was entitled 'Kitchen Sink Drama', and consisted of a washing-up bowl full of soapy water and broken mismatched crockery and cutlery. The former reading room next to the exhibition alcove found a new use as a venue which could be hired out for events and functions.

*

"I see the book club people have made that booking for their murder evening," Tania greeted Jenny as her assistant arrived for work a week later. "So I dare say your friend Emily is pleased and excited."

"Actually," grunted Jenny in response, "she's absolutely gutted."

"How so?" asked Tania, surprised. "From what you were saying, she was looking forward to it."

"She was," sighed Jenny. "But she'd booked a holiday, and the dates clash. The date they've arranged is the only Saturday the organisers had free for, like, months, so the committee grabbed it, and poor Emily's got to miss out. And I hoped she might be able to take me along as a guest, so that's all fallen through as well."

"So, glum faces all round," sympathised Tania.

"Actually, it's not that bad." Jenny brightened up. "The thing is, normally when it's at a hotel, the event takes place over a sit-down dinner, but they can't do that next door because the reading room doesn't have cooking facilities. There's no access to the kitchens. So they've arranged with the Town

Hall catering people to lay on a buffet up in the mayor's parlour, because they're forever doing that for civic do's, via the back staircase. So every so often, between clues, everyone will go upstairs for something to eat, and then come back down and carry on. Emily's put in a word, and the catering people are hiring me as a waitress for the night. So I'll be able to sneak in and see what's going on."

"Better than nothing," nodded Tania. "In fact, much better. Because you obviously get paid, plus you'll be able to enjoy the mystery, and you'll doubtless manage to get yourself a free supper into the bargain. You can report back to me afterwards."

"I'm actually looking forward to it," smiled Jenny. "And you know how much I enjoy a good murder."

"I do," said Tania. "And that being the case, there's a trolley full of returned books there which need to be re-shelved in the Crime section. So, knock yourself out."

Chapter 2

Roland Tighe switched off the mincing machine in the back room of his butcher's shop and gave a small sigh of relief as peace descended on the premises. That would do for now, he thought. The sausages can wait for five minutes. He passed through to the front of the shop, where his teenage apprentice assistant stood moodily surveying the meat display on the main counter.

"Anything exciting happened while I've been back there, Gabe?" he enquired.

"Not really, Mr Tighe." The assistant seemed to come to himself with something of a start. "Two chickens and a pork joint, some liver, and one of those trays of barbecue mix. Oh, and a large steak-and-ale pie."

"Not too bad. Wednesday afternoons are always quiet. No problems?"

Gabe sighed. "Only the usual."

Roland smiled. "Mrs Jenkins again?"

Gabe grunted assent.

"And this time she was complaining about ...?"

"The price of lamb chops. Said as how people aren't made of money, so how do we expect people to pay what we're charging. Outrageous, she called it. And I remembered what you said, about how Welsh salt-marsh lamb is a premium product, but she wasn't having any of it."

"So I'm guessing she didn't buy any?"

"A pound of pig's liver, and that was it."

Roland chuckled. "Well, I'm sure you did your best. Anyway, as we aren't exactly rushed off our feet, I reckon we both deserve a cup of tea. Pop back and put the kettle on. I'll mind the shop."

Tighe's Family Butcher's Shop, located just off

16

Ramston's Market Square, was currently in the hands of the fourth generation of the family. Roland's great-grandfather, the second son of a tenant farmer whose farm lay a few miles outside the town, had been forced to find a means of earning a crust after his own father had made it clear that the precarious state of agriculture meant that only the eldest son would have a chance of making a living off the land. There was no room for the younger man. And so, with his meagre savings, the junior son scraped together enough to purchase two pigs which he butchered himself, and set up a stall at Ramston's weekly market. He was fortunate – he succeeded in selling everything, 'except the squeal', as one of his customers put it, and returned the following week with the produce of three pigs, meeting with equal success. He prospered, acquiring in the process a wife in the shape of the daughter of one of his suppliers, and was eventually able to acquire permanent shop premises, which he handed over to his son before settling into a well-earned retirement in a little cottage on the outskirts of the town. The business carried on through his son and grandson, building a reputation for providing quality meat from local suppliers, and surviving through wars, depressions, and rationing with scarcely a hiccup. And when the grandson, Roland's father, suddenly dropped dead one day, Roland was able to take the reins without difficulty. The only small concern was, there was no fifth generation in prospect. Roland had reached the age of forty-five without ever encountering the right woman, and as the only child of his parents, he was faced with the end of over a century's tradition.

The calendar on the wall opposite the shop

counter caught his eye. Of course – there was this murder evening organised by the Literary Society on Saturday. Mustn't forget that. And he had to admit, he was rather relieved that it replaced the usual monthly meeting, because he was struggling to finish reading the romantic novel which would otherwise have been the subject for discussion by the group. Blasted chick-lit, he thought. Not to his taste at all. He much preferred the grittier type of crime novel, with plenty of blood. Must be something to do with the family heritage, he smiled to himself. And one day, he promised, he really would get round to starting that novel on the subject of a Victorian serial killer, which he'd been turning over in his mind for what seemed like years. Actually starting, that was the problem. Which was what everyone said. He sighed. One day ...

"Here's your tea, Mr Tighe." The voice at his elbow brought him to himself with a start.

"Thanks, Gabe." Roland sipped. "Right. I've got another job for you. Go and get the sausage casings loaded on to the nozzle, and we'll get that next batch of bangers under way."

Gabe laughed. "It's quite funny, Mr Tighe. Sometimes people ask me exactly what goes into our sausages."

"Next time, tell them they don't want to know," replied Roland darkly. "Now, get cracking on those casings."

"Will do, Mr Tighe." Gabe disappeared into the back room and Roland, finishing his tea, followed in his footsteps.

*

Donna McIntosh gave her shoulder-length blonde hair a final brush and gazed closely into the mirror

18

to check that her false eyelashes were on evenly. The huge green eyes that looked back at her were one of her more striking features, among what was generally regarded as a considerable collection. Tall, slim, leggy, attractive, and with a whispering catch in her slightly breathy voice that many an actress would have sold her soul to be able to imitate, Donna was the youngest of the weather presenters on the television station which covered the Wessex region, and probably one of the youngest in the country. The viewing statistics always seemed to twitch upwards slightly whenever she was the one presenting the weather report on the regional lunchtime news or the early evening magazine programme, 'Spotlight Today', and there were rumours that some admirers even stayed up late in the hope of seeing her on the late night bulletin.

Donna would be the first to admit that she was never the most cerebral of her contemporaries at school. And so when, at the age of eighteen, so many of her friends were dispersing, some heading to university at Camford and beyond, while others were shouldering backpacks and departing for the Far East amid tearful and trepidatious farewells from parents, Donna remained in Ramston, securing an undemanding job at the end of a telephone in the customer service call-centre of an insurance company whose headquarters were located on one of the industrial estates on the edge of town. The job almost paid enough to cover the rent of the modest one-bedroom flat which, coupled with the gift from her parents of a small and slightly beaten-up car, gave her a degree of independence, but Donna was able to supplement her finances with an evening waitressing job at

Ramston's trendiest Italian trattoria.

And it was there, one evening, that her fortunes changed. A customer recognised her voice from having spoken to her over the phone about a problem with his car insurance. It was not her professional efficiency which had impressed him so much as the seductive lilt in her speech. To anyone else, that may not have been significant, but the customer concerned happened to be one of the producers at the TV station. To him, what he heard was too good to miss, and having wheedled Donna's contact details out of her, within days he had arranged an audition with the production team of 'Spotlight Today'. All the men on the team were as captivated as the first producer, fully in agreement that the camera loved Donna, while their female colleagues, each with an eyebrow raised, exchanged mute looks of understanding. No matter that Donna's knowledge of meteorology was sketchy at best – a swift course on clicker technique and the use of the autocue, and her screen career as a weather girl was launched. And now, in very short order, at only twenty-three, the one-bedroom flat had become a top-floor apartment in a stylish block, and the modest runabout had been replaced by an open-top sports car in electric blue.

The tap on her dressing-room door heralded the appearance of one of the station's runners. "Five minutes to studio, Donna."

"Thanks, Noah. On my way." A short walk along the corridor, a push of the heavy door which led into the semi-darkness of the outer reaches of the studio, careful avoidance of the cables snaking in all directions across the floor, a quick final check by the make-up man and a swift dab of powder on her nose, and Donna took her place in front of the green screen which, to the viewers at home, displayed the weather map of the region. Autocue rolling, Donna gazed into the large square black eye of the camera and summoned up her trademark bewitching smile. The red light came on.

"Well, who would have thought that the jet-stream would have played such a trick on us?" she announced brightly ...

"And we're out!" came the cry from the unseen control room two minutes later.

"Let me take that for you," said Noah, reaching for Donna's hand-held clicker.

"Thank you, Noah." A gracious smile, and Donna turned, to come face to face with her friend and colleague Alexandra Blaine.

"Lovely as usual," smiled Alex. "I wish I knew how you make it look so easy."

Donna shrugged and gave a Bambi-like blink. "I just say what they tell me to," she replied. "I don't write any of it. Not like you."

Alex laughed. "Oh yes. Me, the great author. That'll be the day. I suppose I'll eventually manage to get past Chapter One of my book. But it's hard going. It's much easier reading them than writing them."

"But you're trying. That's the main thing. And you have to write stuff when you're researching for programmes, don't you?"

"They say anyone can write. They reckon everyone's got a novel in them. I bet you could write a book if you put your mind to it. What about how you came to be working in TV? That's the sort of Cinderella story that people love."

"Mmmm." Donna didn't sound convinced.

"Anyway, you're coming to this Literary Society

21

murder evening on Saturday, aren't you? I'm glad you decided to join. You haven't forgotten, I hope."

"Of course not."

"Well then. You can talk to some of the others. They've encouraged me no end. Maybe they can persuade you to think about writing a book. "Donna's True Story". I bet everyone would enjoy reading that."

Donna gave Alex a sideways look. "Maybe not everyone," she murmured.

*

The flailing arm knocked the insistently-bleeping phone to the floor with a crash, but still the alarm continued to sound. Ivan Ocean opened one bleary eye, pushed himself upright in bed, and reached down, eventually managing to seize the device and still its clamour. "Really?" he mumbled to himself. "Jungian philosophy at ten o'clock in the morning? I don't think so." He rolled over with every intention of going back to sleep.

Ivan was in the third year of his Politics, Philosophy and Economics course at Camford University, with only one year to go. That, however, was possibly the most daunting, since at that point he would have to submit his dissertation, and so far he had not been able to formulate the remotest idea of what the subject matter should be. An extremely bright student at school, Ivan had never seemed to lack ambition, and it had been clear for some time what his preferred path in life would be. Exam grades, very good but not quite as brilliant as his teachers had anticipated, smoothed his path into one of the most sought-after courses at one of the country's most sought-after universities, and there were many prominent figures in public life who had begun their careers in exactly the same way. Membership of the Camford University Union Debating Society was an excellent way for Ivan to hone the skill of public speaking, while securing election to the Student Union's governing body gave him a grounding in administrative skills. In Ivan's case, there was also a chance to put the economics portion of his course to good use when he stood and was elected as the Union's treasurer. The future beckoned – a period as an intern working for a Westminster politician, followed by a short climb up the ladder in local politics, just enough to become noticed, and then candidacy for a parliamentary constituency. Not, obviously, with any immediate prospect of success – it was always necessary to demonstrate your determination by standing as a no-hoper in a seat held safely by your opponent with a massive majority. But once your apprenticeship was served, a winnable seat would eventually come your way, and the glittering path to the top beckoned.

Sadly for Ivan, however, he bore an unfortunate resemblance to a shooting star – brilliant at first, but destined to fade and fall. His was the fate so often experienced by the cleverest pupil in the school. He was so intelligent by comparison with his youthful contemporaries, so quick-witted, that early success came effortlessly to him. In his early years he never had to try, and so he lost the need to do so. The slight fall-off in his scholastic achievements at school seemed to accelerate at university. His submissions were adequate to ensure that he was never in actual jeopardy with his tutors, but occasional eyebrows were raised and murmurs voiced. And it did not help that, egged on by several friends whose presence at

23

Camford owed more to their family backgrounds than their academic abilities, he threw himself increasingly into the social aspect of studentship. A dining club with numerous entitled individuals among its members was a costly drain on his finances, never robust, despite modest subsidies from his parents. Fortunately for him, he found ways to manage. And now, at the age of twenty-one, frequent protracted evenings spent around the countless pubs of the city were more than enough to disrupt Ivan's regular attendance at lectures and tutorials.

"Ivan, my boy," one of his tutors had said in an avuncular moment, surveying a piece of the young man's written work, "this is not quite what I expect of you. There is an unfocussed element to your style of writing. You need to address that. And soon. Your future ... well, let us say that it would be in your best interests."

"What do you propose, sir?" responded Ivan, concerned. His eyes betrayed a hint of panic.

"Let's not worry overmuch," replied the tutor. "I suggest you need some sort of input to your thought processes away from the hothouse of the university."

"Not sure what you mean, sir."

"Join a writers' group. Expose yourself to some differing kinds of expression. You'll probably find all sorts of writing styles, from the sublime to the cor-blimey!" The tutor emitted a quiet chuckle. "You're from Ramston, I think?"

"That's right, sir."

"I thought so. And it just so happens that one of my colleagues, Professor Kates, is a prominent member of their Literary Society. I'm sure a quiet word from me would gain you an introduction.

Have you a car?"

"I do, sir."

"Then it's settled. Distance no problem. Join them, read what they read, write some pieces and put them forward for discussion, and I'm sure the results will prove beneficial."

As Ivan clambered out of bed, he reflected that the tutor's advice had been to an extent useful. He had thought of some ways to improve his writing output, although perhaps not necessarily in the way intended. And his social circle had definitely widened, away from the closeted community of Camford University. His thoughts turned to Donna McIntosh. 'She's fit,' he said to himself. 'And Alex Blaine said in her reminder email she was coming to this Saturday's murder evening. Maybe this is my chance to ask her out.' With that optimistic thought in his mind, he padded towards the shower.

*

Monica de Glenn put down the brush and stood back to survey her work. No – the red wasn't quite right. That would have to be toned down a little. Sharp critical eyes were sure to find fault with it. But a subtle retouch would solve the problem, and once the varnish was on, everything would be as it should.

Monica, in her early forties, was given to wearing long floaty chiffon gowns in tie-dye shades of green and purple, with matching headscarves which did not always succeed in taming her unruly mop of crinkly tawny hair. The large owlish glasses which she affected helped to reinforce the impression of a slightly scatty artistic free spirit, but while the artistic element was accurate, nothing could be further from the truth when it came to scattiness.

The eyes behind the glasses were sharp. Because Monica, in all her ventures, displayed an acute acumen which she did her best to disguise.

She had returned to her roots in Ramston some fifteen years previously, after a fairly mixed personal history. There was a period at art school in London, where her tutors were frequently impressed by her eye for style, technique, and colour. That was where she acquired the somewhat Bohemian image which she never abandoned, as well as adding the 'de' to plain Monica Glenn to create a more artistic aura. Art school was followed by a move to Cornwall, where the pull of the creative community based in and around St. Ives proved irresistible. There she mixed with a variety of kindred spirits – painters, potters, poets, sculptors, fabric designers, all of whose brains she plundered shamelessly in order to garner the widest range of skills. She entered into a torrid relationship with a man twenty years her senior, initially entranced by the exuberance of his free-form animalier bronzes, but the combination of his artistic temperament and his heavy consumption of alcohol led, after one particularly tempestuous argument, to Monica's admission to the local hospital with a broken arm and some spectacular bruises. The injuries healed, but the relationship did not, and Monica made the decision to return home to familiar territory to carve out a solitary but more peaceful existence.

And now, in the picturesque cottage on the edge of Ramston which she had inherited from a dotty but doting aunt, Monica was free to pursue the artistic life in its many forms, and she did not hesitate to do so. Her first love was painting – the walls of the cottage were lined with her early works, while many of her later pieces had found a ready market in small galleries, art shops, and garden centres in the region. And a steady flow of pet portraits, solicited through discreet advertisements in women's magazines and rendered in soft-focussed watercolour, based on photographs submitted by grieving pet-owners whose beloved dogs or cats were no more, provided a regular bread-and-butter income. Her talent for rendering a perfect copy of an image proved highly lucrative in ways she had never expected. But Monica's abilities were not confined to the paintbrush. She had invested in a small kiln in her back garden, tucked away in a wisteria-covered shed, and here she fired small vases in unconventional shapes and sometimes surprising colours, to be sold in the shops where her paintings were displayed. More recently she had turned her hand to the production of small bronze animal sculptures, as a potential alternative to the pet portraits, but her mastery of the lost wax process was still somewhat haphazard. And perhaps inspired by this, her newest venture, and one largely for her own personal pleasure rather than necessarily personal gain, was an attempt at creative writing. A newspaper photograph of Sir Edwin Landseer's Trafalgar Square lions provoked a wry smile when she compared her small bronzes to his monumental creations, and led to a desire to know more about the man. She was surprised to find no biography of him was currently available and, determined on a whim to write one but uncertain of her own writing abilities, she joined the Ramston Literary Society with a view to using her old and well-honed techniques of picking other people's brains. And who knew what opportunities

Saturday's forthcoming murder mystery evening might provide for doing so?

Chapter 3

With a metallic slam, Jack Hughes closed the lid of his wig tin prior to placing it on the top shelf of his locker, before shucking off his gown and placing it on its hanger on the rail beneath. He fumbled with the ties of his bands. How did these damned things always manage to get themselves into a knot, he asked himself, eventually succeeding in untangling them. Off with the waistcoat, undo the top shirt button, and the reflection looking back at him in the robing room mirror finally began to resemble an ordinary human being instead of a barrister. Although the quiet smile of self-congratulation on his face was certainly that of a barrister who had just secured a very satisfactory conviction in a not particularly promising case. He glanced at his watch. Nice quick work by the jury, he thought. Plenty of time for a drink in the 'Wig and Gown' next to the Camford Crown Court, before the drive home to Ramston. But just the one. No sense in tempting fate when the County Constabulary was on one of its regular blitzes against drink-driving.

At the age of thirty-six, Jack was one of the youngest K.C.'s on the Wessex court circuit. His career, if not exactly meteoric, had nevertheless shown a steady progression, and he had been fortunate in the nature of the cases which had come his way. Lucky to secure a pupillage in the chambers of esteemed law firm Putnam Hinder Cage and Lockett, he had worked his way up through the tedium of dull minor embezzlement cases and open-and-shut instances of malicious damage, until one or two trials which made the headlines also made his reputation as a fearsome prosecuting counsel. He decided to apply for silk at what the crustier senior partners in Chambers regarded as a preposterously early age. To their, but not necessarily also his surprise, his application was successful, and a silk gown was his. Now plum cases fell into his lap, and the path to an eventual judgeship seemed clear.

Jack's thirty-six years sat lightly upon him, and his saturnine good looks, thick dark hair which had a habit of flopping forward over his forehead in an attractive way, and his piercing grey eyes, all combined to cause many a heart to flutter among the younger female workers around the Camford courts. And not only the younger staff members. Nor exclusively the females. But it was occasionally remarked upon that he seemed to have no personal private life. Nobody had ever heard mention of a steady girlfriend, although from time to time, whenever there was a formal legal social function, Jack would be seen escorting one of his firm's prettier paralegals, or perhaps a court stenographer. During his after-work drinking sessions in the lounge bar of the 'Wig and Gown' with fellow-barristers from other sets of chambers, he was always affable enough, joining in the superficial banter but never revealing anything in depth about himself.

Leaving the pub on this occasion, he made his way back to the court car park and settled into his silver-grey SUV with its darkened windows for the drive back to Ramston, where he occupied a small town-house in an exclusive gated development on the site of a former brewery in the heart of the town. Arriving home, he threw off his clothes and stepped under the shower, where he luxuriated under the multi-jet hot water for a good ten minutes. Then, wrapping himself in a long heavy silk brocade dressing-gown, and looking every inch the aristocratic young blade from Regency days, he made his way through to his study, where he turned on the computer which he kept for personal use and seated himself in front of it. With the thoughts flowing freely in his head, he felt that now was a good opportunity to carry on with the latest book. With a bit of luck, he might manage to get a couple of chapters under his belt this evening. And what a good idea it had been to join the Literary Society. The writer's block he had encountered while trying to get this second volume under way had not surfaced at all during his creation of the first, and the advice from his fellow members in conquering his problem had been very valuable. And maybe this Saturday's evening of light-hearted murder would inspire thoughts of how to fit a little crime into his writing. You never knew. With a smile, he turned his attention to the activities of his hero.

*

"How's that, Mrs P?"

Mrs Pemberton clasped her hands together in delight, as the soft light from the bobble-fringed shades on the newly-installed wall lamps shed a cosy glow over the sitting room with its Dralon suite, chintz curtains, and clutter of ornaments on every surface. "Oh Ellen," enthused the elderly woman, "that's perfect. I couldn't have asked for better." She blinked away a tear. "That's exactly how my Arthur would have done it if he'd still been with us."

"Then I'm glad he would have approved. And please, do call me Ellie." The young woman climbed down off the stepladder and stood back to survey her work.

"Right then, dear. How much do I owe you?"

"Exactly as I quoted, Mrs P," replied Ellie. "No extras. Now, how would you like to pay? I take cards, or you can do a direct electronic transfer. I'll even take a cheque."

"Oh no, dear," said Mrs Pemberton. "I don't have a credit card, and I'm no use at all with that interweb thing, not at my age. Cash is good enough for me."

"Then it's good enough for me too," smiled Ellie. "And in fact, I'll even knock a fiver off the bill, and we won't bother about paperwork. How does that suit you?"

"That's lovely, dear. Just let me get my handbag."

It often came as a slight surprise to many customers who had booked a job on-line with ED Electrics when they answered the door to a slightly plump overall-clad rosy-cheeked twenty-nine-year-old woman with a beaming smile, hefting a large toolbox. Ellie had never been the most academic pupil at her London comprehensive school, but had always shown a greater aptitude when it came to the more practical subjects. Her skills in the woodwork class were the envy of her male classmates, although they did their best to conceal the fact due to a degree of youthful testosterone-fuelled *amour-propre*. However, they did at the same time adopt her as a kind of unofficial class mascot, and whenever there was any sort of parents' open day at which their work would be displayed, it was always Ellie who was pushed forward to create the object concerned. With no paper qualifications to her name, Ellie was encouraged by her teachers and parents alike to go on to a technical college, where on a sudden whim she made the switch to a course as an electrician. To nobody's surprise, she proved equally adept in this discipline, and emerged from college with a City & Guilds certificate to her name. After serving an apprenticeship for several years, and having secured further qualifications, Ellie reached a cross-roads in her life with the sudden loss of her entire family in a house fire. For many people, the shock and resultant drama would have been crushing, but Ellie refused be beaten, and she decided to launch out on her own. Determined to make a completely fresh start, she moved to Ramston and set up her own business as Ellen Dee, sole trader electrician, and had soon built up a quiet reputation as a reliable and pleasant worker, particularly among her female customers.

"There you are, dear." Mrs Pemberton placed the small wad of notes into Ellie's hand. "And here's another slice of that chocolate cake you enjoyed with your tea." She handed over a foil-wrapped parcel.

"Oh, Mrs P, you shouldn't have," smiled Ellie. "But thank you very much. I'll have it with my supper. And now I ought to be going." With a small amount of juggling, she managed to pick up her toolbox without squashing the cake and made her way out to her little runabout van parked on the drive of Mrs Pemberton's bungalow. She pulled out and, with a final wave, drove away in the direction of her modest terraced house, purchased with her parental legacy, in the jumble of streets that was central Ramston.

Ellie consulted her chunky and slightly mannish watch. Nice early finish for a change, she thought. I can get home and catch up on some paperwork. A slight mental groan. Administration and forms were one of her least favourite parts of her business, but they had to be done to stop the tax man pestering her and taking too close an interest in things. Or – an even better thought, and one which lightened her mood – I can make a cup of tea, sit down with Mrs P's cake, and get to the end of the Society's current book. They're bound to be talking about it in amongst other things on Saturday evening at the murder, and I want to finish it anyway, because I'm desperate to find out whether Alistair and Fiona get together in the end. And I do love a sloppy romance, no matter how some of the other members moan on. So that's me sorted for this evening. Happy once more, she pulled up outside her home.

*

Professor Russell Kates closed the door behind the last of his departing tutorial students with a faint sigh of relief. How on earth some of these young people expect to get through life, when they don't seem to have the faintest idea of how to string two logical thoughts together, is a perpetual puzzle to me, he reflected. Thank goodness I probably won't be around to see what sort of mess they make of the world.

Russell, known as Rusty to a very few highly privileged intimates in the Camford University senior common room, was a tall thin man in his late sixties, with a slightly stooping posture, thinning sandy-coloured hair, and a habit of wearing his half-moon glasses on the end of his nose so that he customarily viewed the world with his head tilted back, giving him a supercilious air. The image was not a misleading one – as one of Camford's more prominent dons, he was highly regarded by many, but unfortunately not least by himself. The reputation was not entirely undeserved. Among his numerous published works, his critique of 'The Philosophy of Tolstoy's Writings' by biographer Warren Peace was regarded as the definitive work on the Russian author's output. His position as a leading member of the university's disciplinary board, covering both students and staff, had been instrumental in gaining him an appointment as a magistrate, where his seat on the bench gave him numerous opportunities to gaze down his nose at the local malefactors who came before him. Many a student had been sent down, and many a petty criminal had received a well-deserved if somewhat harsh sentence, under his steely gaze.

It was his literary reputation that had led to an invitation some years back to become Patron and President of the Ramston Literary Society. Somewhat to his own surprise, he had accepted. That was, he reflected, when the Society had had more grandiose ideas, with pretensions to encourage the higher forms of authorship. In fact, he recalled, wasn't there a local historian who had been involved at one stage? Something about a history of Ramston Abbey. But not, he seemed to recall, one of the finest pieces of writing he had ever encountered. And surely there had been some sort of story involving a murder at the abbey. Russell dismissed the thought. He paid little attention to the local news. So much of it ended up in his court anyway.

And it was unfortunate, but after its first flowering, the Ramston Literary Society seemed to have declined in its ambitions. What had begun as an enterprise to coax the best authorship out of those who may not have realised what talents they possessed, had declined into little more than a common-or-garden book club. True, there were still writers who used it in an effort to improve their style through discussion of other written works, but the majority of the time, it seemed, was spent discussing books of woefully little merit, like the appalling piece of juvenile romantic fiction which was the committee's latest selection. Surely now is the time, thought Russell, to do what I have been thinking about for some while, and wash my hands of the whole sad crew. I've been managing to avoid many of the meetings lately – perhaps this event on Saturday is the ideal opportunity to tell the committee that I am withdrawing. After all, a murder mystery evening! Surely that sums up what depths the Society has sunk to. And in any event, trundling over to Ramston, even on an irregular basis, has become something of a chore. But having promised Professor Whatshisname to introduce his young student to the group, I can't get out of it this time.

But no point, he thought, in leaving them with a sour taste in the mouth. Probably best to indulge in a little light dissembling. After all, there are still one or two members of the Society who show some promise as authors. Perhaps I can maintain contact with them on an informal basis. Yes, that is the best idea. I shall smile and smile, difficult as that may be, and manufacture some plausible excuse as to why I can no longer be involved.

With a nod of satisfaction at a plan successfully constructed, Russell placed the kettle on the gas ring next to the fireplace in his room, and opened a cupboard in search of the caddy containing his favourite Earl Grey tea.

*

"Busy week, Mrs Cash?" enquired the teller behind the counter of the bank on the corner of

Ramston's Market Square, as Caroline placed the canvas bag containing her takings into the well in the counter.

"Not at all bad," replied Caroline with a smile. "But I expect you'll be able to work that out, once you've counted everything to make sure my paying-in slip is correct."

"It always is," said the teller. "Just give me a moment." She headed for the note-counting machine, which was soon giving off a highly satisfying whirr as it performed its function. "Yes, you'll be pleased to know that everything tallies perfectly," declared the returning bank clerk. "And here's your receipt. Any plans for the weekend?"

"Just my usual Saturday stall on the market," said Caroline. "But then," she chuckled, "in the evening, I'm going to be involved with a murder."

"You … sorry, what?" The teller looked and sounded utterly bewildered.

"Don't worry," laughed Caroline. "Not a real one. I'm a member of the town's Literary Society, and we've got a fun murder mystery evening lined up in the old library reading room at the Town Hall. You know – Mrs Smith in the kitchen with the rolling pin, that sort of thing. I'm hoping I'm going to be one of the suspects."

"Oh. Right." The clerk still appeared uncertain. "Well, I hope you enjoy it."

"I'm sure I shall," responded Caroline and, with a cheery wave, emerged on to the Market Square.

Ever since she was very young, Caroline had always had a fascination for the past. Flint arrowheads and cuneiform clay tablets in the tiny museum corner of her junior school had enthralled the small child. Later, she was the only pupil who had not greeted the day's forthcoming history lesson with groans of misery. Her schoolfellows were torn between mockery and admiration at the fact that she was the only one of them who could recite flawlessly the entire list of kings and queens of England, with dates. So it was not to be wondered at that she, at a surprisingly early age, acquired the habit of attending local auctions and, out of her own modest pocket money, purchasing tiny historical treasures such as Roman coins and wooden snuff-boxes. There was only one logical conclusion – on leaving school she set up her own stall at Ramston market, as well as other towns in the vicinity, selling items which she had managed to gather at horrifically early hours at weekend boot sales or auctions at country houses. Eventually, what began as a hobby while she was earning a living on a supermarket checkout became a full-time business, and she was able to open her own business, 'Carrie's Emporium – Antiques, Curiosities, and Collectibles' - in a tiny shop in one of the side streets off the Market Square.

Going hand in hand with her interest in the past had been Carrie's love of historical fiction. For her, sweeping Arthurian romances or Machiavellian Tudor plotting took her into a fascinating other world. She particularly enjoyed the work of one woman author, whose stories of a gum-shoe detective in the days of Imperial Rome amused and delighted her. But her absolute favourites were the writings of Georgina Higher, set in the Regency period, where dashing bucks pursued silk-clad heiresses amidst the dazzle of a court where the main activities were high-stakes gambling and the consumption of vast quantities of champagne. And it seemed to Carrie that, with all her knowledge of the period, surely there was nothing stopping her from trying her hand at writing something similar. Her English examination results at school had always been excellent. Whenever she read something whose punctuation or grammar left a great deal to be desired, she always found herself casting her eyes to heaven and swearing that she could do better. And so, with the desire of achieving her ambition, she had joined the Ramston Literary Society, with the hope of refining her skills and finding a way into the world of authorship.

"I wonder if this murder evening is going to have a historical theme," she said to herself as she made her way back to the shop to prepare the stock for Saturday's market. "I do hope so. I'm sure I could play a very convincing 'Lady Caroline', the duke's daughter." With a quiet smile, she placed the key in the shop door and let herself in.

Chapter 4

"Admit it," said Ron Faye as he placed the cup of tea on his wife's bedside table. "Despite yourself, you're actually intrigued by the whole business."

"I'm not sure I'd go that far," replied Tania. "Although it's been hard to ignore it. I've had Jenny popping over to the library every five minutes this week to let me know the latest on the preparations for this evening."

"I hope the dental health of the citizens of Ramston isn't suffering through her neglect of her duties," grinned Ron, climbing into bed alongside his wife.

"Oh no. Alison would never let her get away with that. She just scoots over between patients, gasps breathlessly a summary of what's happening, and then whips back to the surgery while they still think she's on a loo break."

"She's just excited," remarked Ron indulgently.

"I'm not sure excited covers it. And I can guarantee that I'm going to get no work out of her all day today. I can see myself checking out borrowers with one hand and re-stocking the bookshelves with the other, while at the same time instructing some dear old soul how to use the internet station, as Jenny floats around the place indulging in fantasies involving her playing Miss Lemon to this evening's main detective's Hercule Poirot."

"I'm still actually quite surprised that you're not more enthusiastic about the whole thing," observed Ron. "After all, there's nothing you enjoy more than a good whodunnit. Especially when you're reading last thing at night. In fact, how many have you got stacked up on that bedside cabinet of yours?"

"That's a bit different," responded Tania, a touch defensively. "They're really just chewing gum for the mind to relax my brain before going to sleep. They're not real. No bloody corpse lying there on the ground in front of me. And to be honest, I've had enough genuine murder to last me a lifetime. I hoped the business in Cornwall was just going to be a one-off blip which I could eventually forget all about ..."

"And then, blow me down, what do you get but another real-life murder straight across the road from the library at the abbey," chuckled Ron. "What are the odds?"

"Too high for my liking," retorted Tania. "So I don't think I'm quite ready to think of a murder scene as light entertainment."

"You're surely not worried about the old 'Never two without three' saying, are you?" asked Ron.

"No, of course not," said Tania. "That would be ridiculous."

"Look, why don't you have a word with Jenny and see if she can sneak you in to see what it's all about?" suggested Ron. "Because from everything you've told me she's said, the whole thing is meant to be more comedy than tragedy. It might exorcise a few ghosts. And you never know, you may be converted, and end up fancying going along to one of these murder evenings they run at the Ramston Chase. After all, with your intuitive skills, plus your acting abilities, you'd be a shoo-in to win the prize."

"Flatterer!" Tania gave her husband a good-natured swat. "How desperate are you to win a bottle of bubbly?"

"Utterly," grinned Ron. "Freelance management

consulting has never quite financed the champagne lifestyle it promised."

"Besides, I can't do tonight anyway," pointed out Tania. "Because in case you'd forgotten, I was planning on staying on after the library closed this evening to carry out a stock-check. It's long overdue, and I never get the chance to do it during the day, so that's me booked for the evening. But with luck it may not take too long."

"It had slipped my mind," admitted Ron. "In which case, here's a thought. I've got a bit of work I can steal a march on tonight. When you've finished, why don't we pop in to the Cross Keys for a bite of late supper as a reward for your labours? My treat."

"Lovely," smiled Tania. "I can call you when I'm almost finished."

"Sorted." Ron finished his tea and swung his legs out of bed. "Right. I'm for the shower. Breakfast downstairs in thirty minutes. I'm going all adventurous this morning and trying one of those avocados we bought yesterday, mashed on toast. And then I shall have the pleasure of chauffeuring you to your place of employ."

*

"What do you think?" Jenny Chandler gave a twirl.

"Well," said Tania, looking up from her desk and attempting to stifle a smile, "it's a little over the top, but I'm sure nobody could accuse you of not getting into the spirit of the thing."

Jenny smoothed down the long white apron she wore over the full-length black dress with its leg-of-mutton sleeves. "I borrowed it from Wardrobe at the theatre. Dorothy was actually very nice about it and said I could have it for nothing. I really don't know why some people are so frightened of her. She's always been lovely to me."

"That's because you're relatively new, and you always do what she wants you to do, unlike some of the other members of the society," observed Tania. "She never usually keeps a wardrobe assistant for more than five minutes." She and Ron, being long-time prominent members of the Ramston Operatic And Dramatic Society, had witnessed many a run-in between temperamental performers and the notoriously gruff dragon in charge of the wardrobe department.

"And I know a frock like this isn't actually correct, because apparently this evening's murder isn't a period piece, which is a shame, but I thought a parlourmaid would look right when I'm helping to serve drinks or food at supper time. They do still have parlourmaids in some posh houses, don't they?"

"I'm sure they do," said Tania. "Although you might do better to leave off the mob cap. That may be a bridge too far." She looked at her watch. "And then I think you'd better change back out of that before someone comes into the library and thinks they've strayed into an episode of Downton Abbey, and then you can use the rest of your lunch-break actually to have some lunch."

"Yes, Ma'am." Jenny bobbed a curtsey and, with a giggle, disappeared in the direction of the staff room.

*

"Are you sure you don't mind doing this all on your own?" enquired Jenny anxiously.

"I'm absolutely positive," replied Tania as she headed back to her desk, having ushered the library's final visitor out of the front door and locked it behind them.

"Because I could stay on a bit if it would help."

"No," reiterated Tania firmly. "I have everything under control. It's not as if I haven't done a stock-take on my own before. In fact, I've already made a start on it on the computer this afternoon during a few quiet moments. Besides, Ron and I have everything planned. This won't take forever, and once I've finished here, we're going round to the Cross Keys for some supper. You, on the other hand, have other commitments, and if you don't show your face on time the catering people are going to take a dim view of it. What time are things due to start happening?"

"People are supposed to be turning up from around seven o'clock," said Jenny. "It's going to be drinks beforehand in the art gallery, which I'm meant to be serving, and then things start to happen in the reading room around seven-thirty. And of course, I've got to help setting out the buffet supper in the mayor's parlour beforehand so that it's all ready for the first break. And that means I can sneak into the reading room to watch when things are beginning, and not have to miss much."

"In which case," suggested Tania, "you'd better get a move on. Off you go, and I will cope quite happily on my own."

"All right," agreed Jenny, and started to leave.

"Aren't you forgetting something?" said Tania as her assistant headed for the communicating door which led from the library into the main Town Hall building. "What about that costume of yours?"

"Whoops! Silly me!" Jenny dived into the staff room and reappeared with her parlourmaid's dress in her arms. "I'll forget my head one day," she giggled. The communicating door closed behind her, and Tania, with an indulgent shake of the head, turned to her computer screen.

*

"Red or white, madam?" Jenny tried to keep a straight face as she offered the tray of glasses of wine to the latest arrival through the door of the Town Hall art gallery.

"Oh Jenny, love the outfit!" laughed Alex Blaine as she surveyed her friend. "Bit different from your Zumba kit."

"Just getting into character," replied Jenny with an answering smile. "Besides, I'm not sure anyone here needs to see me in Lycra this evening."

"True. It might distract them from their detecting activities." Alex took a glass. "By the way, I don't think you know Lindsey." She gestured to the man at her side.

"No, I don't think I do." Jenny arched a speculative eyebrow.

"Lindsey Doyle." The man extended a hand which Jenny, after a moment's juggling with her tray, shook. He was above medium height, with matinée idol looks, an impressive tan, and a set of dazzling teeth which Jenny estimated, with an instant professional assessment, must have cost several thousand pounds. "How do you do?"

"I do very well," breathed Jenny, neglecting to let go of the hand. "Alex, you never told me ..."

Alex seemed highly amused. "Lindsey is my colleague at the TV station," she declared. "He's one of our sports reporters. Cricket correspondent, actually. He's just come along as my plus-one for the evening. And that's all, really." She leaned in close to Jenny. "Worse luck."

"Alex has saved me from an evening's boredom sitting at home on my own," explained Lindsey. "Roderick's away at a medical conference in

45

Amsterdam this weekend, and Alex thought a little light murder might take my mind off whatever he might be up to, knowing that city's reputation."

"Rubbish," retorted Alex. "You know you two are the perfect couple. It's more than his life's worth to be a bad boy. I'd certainly have words with him. Anyway, we should mingle. We're holding up the queue, and I can see Donna McIntosh over there. I hope she's ready to be a suspect."

"How do you mean?" asked Jenny.

"The organisers got in touch with me for a bit of background on our people so they can decide who's going to be what character. Helps with the fun, they say. I wonder what they've chosen for Donna. Let's go and have a chat to her." The two moved away.

"I'm surprised to see you here, professor. I didn't think this was your kind of thing at all." Annette Curtin looked up quizzically from her diminutive five foot height at the lofty visage of Russell Kates, who was casting an eye over a portrait of a rather stodgy-looking former mayor of Ramston.

"Good evening, Annette," replied Kates. "No, you're probably right. I wouldn't normally attend this kind of event. But I had a particular reason for coming this evening."

"Oh yes?" Annette's beady eyes brightened. The bird-like elderly woman radiated an air of excited curiosity. "And what might that be, I wonder."

"I think I'll keep that to myself, if you don't mind, Annette. Although I know you like to be aware of absolutely everything that's going on."

Annette drew herself up, insofar far as she was able. "Merely taking an interest in other people, I'm sure," she replied in offended tones. "Well, I shall leave you to whatever it is that you're doing." She marched away with a dismissive sniff.

"Ready for an evening of blood and guts, Roland?" enquired fellow shopkeeper Caroline Cash. "Although I don't suppose that represents much of a change for you." She laughed.

"I don't expect we'll get any actual blood, Carrie," responded Roland Tighe with an answering smile. "Although it wouldn't bother me if it did. But I suspect the whole thing is going to be a bit more sedate than that. We'll see."

"How's that serial killer idea of yours coming along?"

Roland sighed. "Still thinking it through. But you never know – I might pick up a few tips this evening."

"How are we doing, ladies?" Jack Hughes joined Ellie Dee and Monica de Glenn who were murmuring together at one side of the room. "Plotting tactics for this evening, or planning your next literary blockbuster?"

"Neither, actually, Jack," replied Monica. "In fact, we were discussing the fact that one of this evening's organisers has sidled up to each of us and asked us if we'd be participants in tonight's murder."

"Really?" Jack laughed. "In that case, you're probably going to need a good lawyer. Don't forget me, will you?"

"We're not actually meant to say anything yet, Monica," said Ellie. "But I suppose we can tell you, Jack, as long as you don't spread it around. We've both been given a character to play, although I think mine really ought to have been given to that Donna McIntosh over there."

"Why's that?"

"You really shouldn't say any more, Ellie," stated

Monica. "It'll all come out soon enough."

"That's what worries me," muttered Ellie.

"Um ... hello." Ivan Ocean cleared his throat diffidently. "I don't think I've seen you at a meeting before, have I?"

Donna McIntosh turned her Bambi eyes to the slightly blushing young man at her shoulder. "No, I've only just joined. My friend Alex persuaded me to come. She thinks I ought to write a book about my life. I'm ..."

"I know who you are," interrupted Ivan. "I've seen you on TV. Loads. I think you're very good. And I'd read your book."

"Aren't you sweet," dimpled Donna. "But I'd have to write it first. And I'm not sure ..."

"Oh, everyone here is very encouraging. They all say so. Maybe we could have a chat later." Ivan gave a hopeful smile. "Over a drink?"

"Er-hem!" The loud clearing of the throat of the slightly plump young man in an ill-fitting suit, standing in the doorway of the reading room, stilled the conversation and drew the attention of the dozen or so people scattered around the art gallery amongst the alcoves formed by the former bookshelves, some seated chatting, some browsing the art on display. "Ladies and Gentlemen! May I have your attention please? I'm sorry to interrupt, but I have some very grave news for you. I have to tell you that there has been ... a murder."

The announcement was greeted with a small ripple of reaction and an exchange of glances between those present.

The young man was obviously not satisfied with the result of his announcement. "I'm sorry, ladies and gentlemen, but I do not think you have fully comprehended the shocking nature of what I have just said. So I have to repeat myself – there has been …" A large intake of breath. "A MURDER!"

This time the reaction was obviously closer to what was required, as the guests produced a selection of exaggerated gasps of astonishment and horror, which rapidly turned into a general round of laughter.

"Now that's rather more like it," smiled the young man. "Although I should remind you, ladies and gentlemen, that murder is no laughing matter. Now I believe that you will all be able to assist in solving this murder, and therefore I would ask you all if you would proceed through here into our interview room and take your seats around the table." He stood aside from the reading room door and indicated that everyone should enter. Amid intrigued murmurings, the members of the Ramston Literary Society passed through into the reading room, where individual pieces of furniture had been pushed together to form a refectory-style table down the centre of the room. The speaker followed behind the last person before closing the door and joining another slightly older man at the far end of the room, while Jenny took her place standing unobtrusively in one corner. "Thank you, ladies and gentlemen. Now let me introduce myself. I am Detective Sergeant Nick Ewall, and the gentleman standing alongside me is my guv'nor, Detective Inspector Willy Evertwigg. Inspector Evertwigg is the senior investigating officer, and as such, he will be conducting this evening's investigation. Sir?" He stood back to allow his fellow to step forward..

"Good evening, ladies and gentlemen," began the other. He was tall and dark, somewhere around forty, and wearing a considerably smarter suit than his colleague. He exuded an air of confidence and command. "Now, as my sergeant here has said, there has indeed been a murder, and I have reason to believe that the murderer is ... in this very room!" He surveyed the assembled company with an encouraging look, and after a brief moment, those present picked up their cue and produced an appropriate reaction. "That's better," smiled the 'inspector'. "I see we begin to understand one another. So let me tell you what we know of the case so far.

"The victim of this shocking murder is a young woman by the name of Shirley Knott. She was a reporter on the local newspaper, and fairly notorious as the town gossip. And I have reason to believe that she was known to each and every one of you, and it appears that she was in possession of some information which has caused one of the people here to bring about her early demise. Her dead body was discovered under highly suspicious circumstances, and I shall be revealing details of this as soon as I receive the forensic report." He turned to his colleague. "Sergeant, do we know when we shall have that available?"

"I shall be collecting it shortly, sir," replied the 'sergeant'.

"Excellent. Now, as the evening progresses, I shall be revealing certain facts about the deceased and her activities, as well as showing you various clue items which have come into my possession. You will have an opportunity to examine these during breaks in the proceedings. I shall also, from time to time, be interviewing a number of witnesses who should be able to contribute to our knowledge of the case. And finally, once all is known, I shall be enlisting your assistance in identifying the culprit.

You each have been provided with a notepad, together with a form to fill in at the end of proceedings with your solution to the crime. Is that all clear?"

Nods and murmurs of agreement from around the room.

"Now you may all have noticed that my sergeant here was unobtrusively circulating among you when you first arrived, and he has in fact been able to identify eight of you who are the principal suspects in this case. He has also given each of the eight a card containing a brief statement, which I would ask you to stand up in turn and read out for the group." An exchange of looks of mild surprise around the table among those who were unaware of what had happened. "So perhaps we could go around the table, starting on my left. And don't forget – everyone has a guilty secret."

Chapter 5

The words of the 'inspector' seemed to produce an unaccountable nervous chill among those present. But after a moment, one person got to their feet.

"I suppose I'd better kick things off then," said Jack Hughes. He cleared his throat dramatically and held a small laminated card out in front of him. "*My name is Rory Lyons,*" he read. "*I am an animal keeper at the local zoo, in charge of the big cats. And I was acquainted with Shirley Knott because she came to the zoo to cover a story about one of our cheetahs having cubs. She said she was very interested in cheetahs.*" He resumed his seat.

"Oh, I say, that's very clever," chirped Annette Curtin. "'Rory Lyons', and he's in charge of the lions at the zoo! That's very funny."

"If you wouldn't mind, madam," said the 'inspector' severely. "We have several people to hear from, so if we could refrain from comment until everyone has finished. May we have the next suspect, please?"

As Annette adopted an expression of mock apology, the next person stood.

"*Hello,*" read Caroline Cash. "*I'm Anne Teak, and I own a jewellery business in town. I met Shirley Knott because she came to my shop to have a family heirloom valued. She seemed very interested in my stock, particularly some of the more valuable items, and said she would like to come and interview me on the subject of Victorian jewellery.*"

Annette couldn't help herself. "'Anne Teak'," she whispered, nudging her neighbour. "How do they think these names up?" At a further stern look from the 'inspector', she subsided once more.

"My turn, I think." Roland Tighe rose to his feet. He fished in his jacket pocket for a pair of glasses and peered at the card in his hand. "Here goes. '*My name is Justin Case, and I am an insurance salesman for the Acme Insurance Company based here in town. I encountered Shirley Knott when I was carrying out a campaign of door-to-door sales calls, and she told me that, as a reporter, she had heard stories of old people being mis-sold unsuitable life insurance. Naturally I told her I knew nothing of such things.*"

There was a pause. "Oh. Is it me?" Donna McIntosh got reluctantly to her feet. "I don't know if I can ..."

"It's fine, Donna," spoke up Alexandra Blaine alongside her. "Just think of the card as your autocue. And you're so used to speaking to millions of people when you do your weather reports, so just these few should be a doddle."

Donna gave a wan smile. "All right." She held her card out in front of her. "*I am Hannah Condor, and I am a ... a herpetologist.*" She broke off. "Oh, that's not very nice. Does that mean I have herpes? I don't like this."

"That's not what it means at all, dear," said Annette. "It just means you're a scientist who specialises in snakes."

"I knew somebody would get that wrong," hissed the 'sergeant' to the 'inspector' out of the side of his mouth.

"Do carry on, miss," said the 'inspector' through slightly gritted teeth, ignoring his colleague.

Donna took another deep breath. "*I am a herpetologist, and I also work at the zoo, carrying out research into rare snake venoms.*" She gave a little laugh of relief. "Oh, I see. I get it now. Sorry.

53

Where was I? Oh yes. *… snake venoms. And Shirley Knott contacted me because she'd heard stories of human testing that went wrong, and she wanted to write a story about it.*"

Annette Curtin attempted to control a small explosion of mirth, but without success. "'Hannah Condor'! Who makes these up?"

"All rise!"

Everyone looked with some astonishment at Russell Kates.

"Apologies, everyone," said the university don. "I was simply attempting to inject a small note of seriousness into the proceedings. It seemed appropriate in view of my character." He stood. "*If it please the court. My name is Lord Loverduck, and I am a judge on the judicial circuit which includes this town. I was approached by Miss Knott as she was pursuing a story concerning certain alleged miscarriages of justice which are said to have occurred while I was sitting. Naturally, I was unable to comment.*"

"*What an amazing co-incidence.*" Monica de Glenn was the next to rise and speak. "*Because I was also approached by Shirley Knott in connection with the very same story. I am Evelyn Hall, and I am a former police officer. Shirley Knott said that she had heard that there were questions regarding the arrest record at my station, but I decided to take early retirement, so these were never investigated. But she said there was still work to be done.*" As she sat down, she murmured to the person alongside her, "This is all getting very interesting."

"I think it must be me next," announced Ivan Ocean, getting to his feet. He cast a look in the direction of Donna McIntosh, hoping to catch her eye, but was disappointed to see that she was preoccupied with studying her fashionably-decorated fingernails. "Right." He looked at the card in his hand. *"My name is Aidan Comfort, and I am a nurse in the palliative care department of the town's Royal Hospital. Shirley Knott came into our department asking questions about the apparently early deaths of some of our patients, but we told her that there was no truth in any of the rumours she had heard, and she would need to contact the hospital authorities before she carried out any further intrusions."* He resumed his seat after another fruitless attempt to gain Donna's attention.

"Looks as if it's just me left," declared Ellie Dee. She stood. "Well, here goes. *I am Anna Royd, and I am a meteorologist at the local television company."* She looked along the table. "I said they should have given this character to Donna. What do I know about the weather?"

"Please, miss, if you wouldn't mind continuing," urged the 'inspector'.

"Oh, okay. *Shirley Knott got in touch with me because there had been an accident at a local fête, and a child was injured when a bouncy castle blew away. She wanted me to comment, and said there were serious questions to be asked about my professional competence after I had produced a weather forecast for that day saying that the winds would be light."*

The 'inspector' stepped up to the head of the table. "Thank you, ladies and gentlemen, for those initial statements. I'm sure they have given everyone food for thought. And in case you were not able to take full notes of what was said, you will be pleased to have a transcript of all statements, which will be laid out for you to collect from the evidence table which will be situated in the next room." He gestured towards the art gallery. "And now, on the subject of food, I believe it is time for you to have some refreshments to help you to digest what you have heard so far. So if you would like to follow this young lady ..." He pointed to Jenny. "... she will conduct you there."

Jenny moved towards the door. "This way, please. We're going up to the mayor's parlour where your first course is ready." She led the way through the art gallery and out into the main entrance hall of the building, and onwards up the stairs to where the door to the mayor's parlour stood open on the landing.

*

"Ladies and gentlemen." The 'inspector' appeared in the doorway of the mayor's parlour just as the catering supervisor and Jenny were about to remove the last of the empty canapé and vol-au-vent platters. "If you have quite finished, we are ready to resume our investigation down in the interview room, so if you would like to take your places ..."

"We'd better be quick," muttered Jenny to the supervisor. "I don't want to miss anything. It's all quite exciting."

"Don't worry," replied the supervisor. "I'll take these down the back stairs to the kitchen, and then I'll bring up the food for main course. It's only quiches and some salads, so I can easily do it on my own. I'll leave everything covered so that you can just whip the cling film off when they all next come up. You can see to the glasses of wine. And the dessert for the third break is only some gateaux, which are already sliced, so I'll do the same there. I can easily manage by myself, and once I've brought those up I can slide off early. So you go and enjoy yourself."

"Are you sure?" demurred Jenny.

"Go!" smiled the supervisor, and Jenny scampered away to join the last of the participants as they descended the main stairs and made their way into the reading room.

"You will be pleased to hear," announced the 'inspector', once everyone had resumed their seats, "that we have made further progress in the case, and that my sergeant has managed to track down a witness, whom I am about to interview." He raised his voice. "Would the witness like to come in here please."

The door from the art gallery opened to admit an elderly man with a shock of white hair and a large walrus moustache, dressed in baggy overalls, and sporting an apron liberally stained with black ink. He wore thick pebble glasses.

"Please come forward, sir. Now would you please introduce yourself."

"My name is Lloyd - Tab Lloyd. I am in charge of the printing presses of the town's newspaper," said the man. An amused chuckle arose from those present as they realised that the witness was none other than the 'sergeant' in heavy disguise.

"And were you familiar with the deceased, sir?" enquired the 'inspector'.

"Oh no, nothing like that," protested the supposed printer. "My missus would give me hell if there was anything of that sort going on."

The 'inspector' gave a mock sigh of exasperation. "No, I mean, did you know the dead woman, Shirley Knott?"

"No, honestly, she would, really, my missus. But as for that Shirley, she was a one. Always poking her nose into things that didn't concern her. I could tell you some tales."

"Excellent, Mr Lloyd. That's just what I wanted to hear." The 'inspector' addressed the room. "And perhaps, ladies and gentlemen, you might like to take notes of any information which you may consider helpful."

The interview proceeded, with notes being hastily scribbled as facts were revealed that might have some bearing on the case, each 'suspect' being shown to have a plausible motive for murder. Finally, the witness was dismissed, and left the room to a generous round of applause.

"And now," continued the 'inspector', "I have some further facts to reveal to you. I have here ..." He brandished a document. "... an extract of the post-mortem report which shows how the deceased met her end. I also have a note, apparently in the deceased's own writing, which makes unspecified threats to disclose embarrassing facts in the event of non-cooperation by the person to whom it was written. Unfortunately, that note was unaddressed, and was found next to Ms Knott's body. We are therefore not sure whether the note was about to be passed to its intended recipient, or whether the recipient confronted Ms Knott with it during an encounter which had fatal results. And finally, among other items, there is an antique police truncheon, dating from the nineteenth century, which appears to show traces of blood, although at this stage we do not know whose. You may like to draw your own conclusions. All these items will be placed on the evidence table in the adjoining room for you to examine at your leisure. And in order to allow you to do this, we will take another break in proceedings, as I believe further refreshments are available for you upstairs." He looked at his watch. "We shall reconvene in forty-five minutes."

*

"Jenny." Alexandra Blaine stopped her friend as she was circulating with a tray of wineglasses. "I have to say that this was a brilliant idea of yours. I'm enjoying it very much."

"Me too," enthused Jenny.

"Even though you're having to work?" enquired Lindsey Doyle.

"Oh, it's not so bad," replied Jenny. "In fact, I think I'm getting the best deal out of everyone. I get paid for doing it, and I get a free supper ..."

"Don't think I didn't notice you sneaking off behind the door to have a quick nibble," smiled Alex.

"... and I get to enjoy the murder which you lot are paying for," finished Jenny triumphantly.
"I'm definitely going to book to go their next one at the hotel. As long as it's not the same plot, that is."

"No, they've got several," Alex reassured her. "What I admire is the way they think up all these different motives for the characters." She laughed. "I mean, some of them are pretty obvious, like Carrie Cash playing a dodgy jeweller. Mind you, I'd hate to think that might be too close to the truth for comfort. But as for Roland Tighe playing an insurance salesman? I could easily see him as a mad abattoir butcher running amok with a cleaver. How many insurance salesmen have actual blood on their hands?"

"Probably more than we ever suspect," smiled Lindsey. He looked around the room. "And by the way, where is everybody? We seem rather thin on the ground."

"I think some people went downstairs to have

59

another look at the clues," said Alex. "And last time I saw Donna she said she was going to the loo. I'm not sure she's having the best time. She seems nervous, although I can't think why."

"Playing to a real audience instead of just the red eye of the camera?" hazarded Lindsey. "But I'll tell you one person who seems to be enjoying themselves."

"Who's that?"

"That older lady – I can't remember who she is."

"Oh, that's Annette Curtin. Yes, she's taking it all in." Alex lowered her voice and looked around. "Just checking she's not lurking, because she has a habit of popping up right next to you. And in fact, she'd have been perfect casting for the late and not-so-lamented Shirley Knott. She knows everyone's business. She'll probably get murdered herself one day."

Lindsey checked his watch. "Shouldn't we getting back to it soon? I haven't seen that inspector chap for ages."

"Oh, he and his sergeant are down in the kitchen having their own supper," reported Jenny. "They sneaked off down the back stairs to have something to eat while you lot were in here."

"In fact, talk of the devil," said Alex. "Here's Inspector Evertwigg now." The 'inspector' was just emerging through the door from the back stairs, wiping final crumbs from around his mouth. "Inspector, are you summoning us for the next segment?"

"I shall be in a moment, madam," replied the 'inspector'. "I've just sent my sergeant off to track down another witness for me to interview."

"I can't imagine who that could be," laughed Lindsey. "But we did enjoy his first incarnation, so

I'm looking forward to his second."

"I can't think what you mean, sir," smiled the 'inspector' in response. "But if you'll excuse me, I shall spend a few minutes circulating among your fellow detectives to see if they have any questions, and then we can resume."

"I'll get the remains of the food cleared," said Jenny, and briskly set about the task of removing platters and bowls.

After a few moments, she joined the rest of the party downstairs in the art gallery, where people were dotted about in ones and twos, some in conversation with the 'inspector', who looked around and announced, "Ladies and gentlemen, let's continue." He made his way to the closed doors of the reading room and threw them open, to reveal the figure of Russell Kates seated in his place, slumped over the table. "Please, sir," he said, moving forward. "If you don't mind, I think we'd rather stick to our own script rather than improvising."

There was no reaction, and the 'inspector' placed his hand on Russell's shoulder, suspecting that the don might have dozed off. After a moment, he stepped back and turned to the others, a look of horror on his face. "Oh my god! Somebody call the police. I think … I think he's dead!"

Chapter 6

The communicating door into the library from the Town Hall burst open, and a breathless Jenny Chandler erupted through it, just as Tania Faye had closed down her computer and was reaching for the bank of light switches.

"Thank goodness I've caught you," gasped Jenny.

"Another minute and you wouldn't have," replied Tania, slightly taken aback by the other's distraught state. "What's up? Where's the fire?"

"No fire," responded Jenny. "But ... there's been a murder!"

Tania laughed. "I thought that was the whole idea of this evening. Although I must say, aren't you taking this getting-into-character thing a bit far?"

"No, you don't understand," insisted Jenny. "There's actually been a murder. A real one. There's a body in the library – well, the old reading room, that is."

Tania couldn't quite take it in. "This isn't some elaborate joke, is it, Jenny? A twist in the plot to draw me in as some sort of external investigator?"

Jenny took a deep breath and forced herself to speak calmly. "Honestly, Tania. I wouldn't joke about it. I've actually seen the man, and they reckon he's really dead. It's one of the members of the Literary Society. And somebody said they were going to call the police and we should all stay exactly where we were, but I couldn't think straight, and my only thought was to come and find you. So I did."

At that moment, Tania's mobile rang. "Hello, Ron."

"Hello, love. Your text said you'd be here in two minutes. Dennis is just finding us a table."

"I'm afraid you'll have to tell Dennis Dean that supper at the Cross Keys is going to need to be put on hold."

"Why? What's up?"

"It looks as if there's been a murder over here."

A chuckle. *"Well, no surprise there. I thought that was what this Literary Society evening was all about. Don't tell me they've dragged you into it."*

"No, this is the real thing, by the sound of it. Jenny's come rushing through from the Town Hall in a state. She says someone's dead. I think I'd better go through and find out what's going on, since I'm probably the senior council employee on the premises."

"Not on your own, you don't. I'm on my way." Ron disconnected abruptly.

Tania turned to Jenny. "One minute." She moved to ensure that the library front door was locked, and then switched all the main lights off, leaving only the security lights shedding their dim glow over the room. Gathering up her bag and coat, she led the way to the connecting door to the main Town Hall building, Jenny trailing in her wake. "Right," she said in firm tones, her hand on the door handle. "Show me."

The pair passed through into the Town Hall foyer, just as Ron Faye pushed his way in through the front entrance. "What's all this about, love?" he asked, panting slightly, having evidently run across the Market Square in something of a hurry.

"That's what I'm about to find out," replied Tania. "Jenny?"

The young woman stepped through the doorway to the art gallery, to reveal knots of people standing about, some murmuring among themselves, some in solitary silence with shocked

63

expressions on their faces. Ignoring them all, Jenny opened the door to the reading room and gestured towards the still figure lying slumped across the table at the far end of the room, his head at an odd angle. Tania and Ron swiftly advanced and peered at Russell Kates' inert form.

"We can't really tell for sure without touching him, which I'm not about to do," muttered Ron to his wife, "but he looks pretty dead to me. Puts me in mind of that chap in Cornwall."

"Don't remind me," said Tania. "But I think you're right. We'd better leave everything exactly as it is and shut the room back up until the police get here."

The couple returned to the art gallery and closed the door firmly behind them, just as the strident tones of a police siren could be heard arriving outside the building. The sound ceased, and within seconds a middle-aged woman with short iron-grey hair strode though into the Town Hall foyer, attended by a younger man who looked as if he couldn't have been long out of school. "Who's in charge here?" she demanded.

"I am." Two voices were raised simultaneously, as both Tania and the individual playing 'Inspector Evertwigg' stepped forward. The two looked at each other in mutual surprise.

"Well, that's a good start," remarked the woman, sarcasm plain in her voice. "But in any event, as of now, I am." She produced a warrant card. "I'm Detective Inspector Marion Bright, and my colleague here is Sergeant Miner." She looked in turn at the two who had spoken, before her eye fell on Tania. "And who are you?"

"I'm Tania Faye. I'm Head Librarian at the town library, and I was working late in the main library in another part of the building when I heard what had happened. As far as I know, I'm the only council management staff member present. Which I suppose makes me the most responsible person here at the moment. And this is my husband Ron."

The detective's attention turned to the 'inspector'. "Well, who's this then?"

"I'm Inspector Willy Evertwigg ..."

"What?" barked the detective.

"That's to say," floundered the other, "I'm really Sam Farley, playing Inspector Evertwigg." He gestured to his colleague alongside him, currently dressed in a loud striped shirt, red braces, and enormous spectacles, with shiny slicked-back hair. "And this is Mike Standon, but at the moment he's cub reporter Jimmy Wilson. Although he's normally Nick Ewall." The detective screwed up her face in bewilderment. "Sorry, it's a bit confusing. Because we're doing this murder here this evening."

The detective's face was a picture. "Are you telling me that you're confessing to murder?"

"No!" blurted Sam hastily. "No. I mean we're doing a fun murder mystery evening here tonight for the Ramston Book Club, or whatever they are."

"Fun?" growled the detective. "Do you mean this is some kind of false alarm? Are you trying to tell me that there hasn't been an actual murder?"

"Oh no, I'm afraid there has," intervened Tania. "We should have said straight away. You see, there's a body in the library."

The detective took a deep breath and gave Tania a long level look. "A body in the library?" she echoed slowly, eyebrows raised in incredulity. She seemed to be making a strenuous effort to remain calm.

"Yes," nodded Tania. "Well, the old library reading room, anyway. Would you like me to show you?"

"I think that would be a very good idea, Mrs … Faye, did you say?" replied Inspector Bright through gritted teeth.

"It's through here." Tania led the way into the reading room, followed by the two police officers, with Ron bringing up the rear, as the others all crowded into the doorway, necks craning and mouths open. Tania gestured to the figure of Russell Kates. "I'm afraid my husband and I have already been in here to check on what we'd been told by my assistant, who's working here tonight. But we haven't touched anything, I assure you."

"Good," grated the detective. "That's something, at least." She stepped alongside the body and took a brief look before announcing, "Well, it's certainly not a false alarm. And that looks suspiciously like a wound to the back of his head," she mused to herself, "so natural causes seem to be ruled out." She thought for a moment before turning to her junior colleague. "Right, Miner," she snapped briskly. "I want the doctor here straight away, and then you can get SOCO here pronto. Tell them we have a suspicious death. In the meantime," she added, looking at the group clustered at the room's entrance, "everybody out! And that door is to be kept shut. This room is now a crime scene. And you are all to remain here until I find out what is going on." She shooed everyone back into the art gallery.

"What are we supposed to do now, inspector?" Lindsey Doyle stepped forward, exuding an air of calm which was noticeably absent from many of those present.

"And you are, sir, …" asked Bright.

"My name is Lindsey Doyle, inspector." The sports reporter seemed faintly surprised that his statement aroused no flicker of recognition. "You might have seen me on television." Still no reaction. "But the thing is, I'm here with my colleague from the TV station, who is secretary of the Ramston Literary Society. And I imagine she is best placed to explain tonight's situation." He indicated Alex standing at his side. "Alex, perhaps you can help the inspector."

"About time somebody did," muttered the detective. She looked around the gallery. "For the moment, I want everyone to take a seat. I shall want a statement from each of you. In the meantime ..." She drew Alex aside into one of the alcoves where a pair of chairs was located. "So, tell me, Miss ...?"

"Blaine. Alexandra Blaine. As Lindsey said, I'm the Society's secretary, so I was the one mainly responsible for organising this evening."

"Good." Bright looked up as her sergeant appeared at the entrance to the alcove.

"Everyone's on their way, boss."

"In that case, Miner, you can take some notes here. First things first, Miss Blaine. Who is the dead man?"

"His name's Professor Russell Kates. He's one of our most senior members. He's some sort of academic at the University of Camford."

"And what happened?"

Alex shrugged. "I don't know. You see, we were having this murder evening ..."

"Stop right there," interrupted the detective. "Explain."

"It's one of our social events," said Alex. "We have them from time to time, and somebody suggested

67

we have a murder mystery evening, like they do at some hotels."

"I've heard of that," butted in the sergeant. "They do them at the Ramston Chase. They sound like fun. I've been wanting to take my girlfriend to one."

"Yes, thank you for that, sergeant," said Bright drily. "So, carry on."

"It's organised by the chap you were speaking to earlier," continued Alex. "He runs a business – 'Murder At Your Place', it's called. We all get together, and they say there's been a murder which we're all supposed to help solve. And we're all given different characters to play, and we get clues, and there's a supper served during the evening."

"So this professor chap, he was supposed to get murdered?"

"No," stated Alex. "That's what's so horrible. The fictitious murder in the story has already taken place, so it doesn't happen during the evening. It's just described. But the whole story was playing through, and every so often we broke to go up to the mayor's parlour upstairs to have supper. But when we came down after the main course ..." She broke off, and her hand went to her mouth.

"Yes?" encouraged the detective.

"We all went back into the room and ... he was just there. Lying across the table. And the inspector ... I mean the one in the game ... went to look at him, and said he was dead. And so someone phoned 999, and ... here you are."

Bright reflected for a moment. "You say you all went back into this reading room? So you're saying everyone was all together at this time?"

"Yes. Well ... I mean, no."

The detective's gaze hardened. "So which is it? Yes or no?"

Alex shrugged helplessly. "When the previous bit of the investigation finished, the inspector ... I mean the one playing the inspector ..."

"You mean Mr ..."

"Farley, ma'am," prompted Sergeant Miner.

"Thank you, sergeant. Carry on, miss."

"Mr Farley said that it was time for everyone to go upstairs for the main course of supper, so we all left together."

"Including Professor Kates?"

"I think so, yes. And then we were all upstairs getting our food, but then people seemed to go off in different directions. I think some people took the chance to go to the loo, and a couple of people were going to nip outside for a cigarette. One or two went back for seconds. Someone said they were going to come down and have a look at the evidence ..."

"What evidence is this?" demanded Bright.

"The evidence in the murder mystery," explained Alex. "There's a table just round the corner in one of the other art gallery alcoves with copies of the suspects' statements and clues and weapons and so on. They were there for people to remind themselves of what had happened in the story so far."

"And can you remember who was where?"

Alex gave a troubled shrug. "No, not really."

"Hmmm," grunted the detective. She stood. "Show me this so-called evidence table." She followed Alex to another of the alcoves, where two smaller tables had been pushed together to display a scatter of printed documents, together with a selection of items relevant to the evening's murder story – a silver spirits flask, the torn half of a hand-written note, a syringe, a yellow household glove, a necklace which looked as if it purported to be diamonds, an antique police truncheon, a wicked-looking oriental dagger, and a small blue bottle labelled 'Poison'. Bright peered closely at the last few. "Miner," she snapped, "Get this area cordoned off. Put some chairs across the entrance until SOCO get here. Nobody is to come near. We may have our murder weapon." She stepped back into the central area of the gallery and raised her voice. "Your attention please, everybody. I need this room cleared, but you are all to remain in the building until we have your statements." She addressed Tania. "Mrs Faye, I assume you know the building. Is there somewhere everyone can wait?"

"How about back upstairs in the mayor's parlour?" suggested Tania.

"Good. Everybody, please follow Mrs Faye's suggestion and adjourn upstairs. Miner, escort them please."

Amid murmurings, the party moved back into the Town Hall foyer and climbed the stairs once more, seating themselves at the various supper tables around the room while exchanging uneasy glances, leaving Inspector Bright alone with Tania and Ron.

"There's really no need for you two to remain," said the inspector. "As you plainly weren't on the premises when the murder occurred, you do not qualify as witnesses, and I see no reason to keep you here."

"Thank you, inspector," replied Ron.

"I just wonder ..." said Tania hesitantly.

"Yes, Mrs Faye?"

"I just wonder if I might be able to help you in some way, inspector. You see, the thing is ..."

"Oh good grief!" interrupted Bright. She let out a snort of impatience. "I thought that name rang a bell. Mrs Tania Faye, the amateur librarian sleuth. You were involved with that murder case at Ramston Abbey, weren't you?"

"I may have made one or two suggestions to Inspector Copper," admitted Tania modestly.

"Yes. I remember hearing all about that from him," said Bright. "He tells quite the story."

"By the way, where is Inspector Copper?" asked Ron. "We might have expected to see him this evening."

"Away on a firearms course," responded Bright shortly. Tania could have sworn she heard the detective add 'Lucky man' under her breath. "So you have me. I, however," she continued with some force, "do not think that I shall be needing you. We have considerable professional resources at our disposal. So please, Mr and Mrs Faye, do not involve yourselves with this case. I suspect you would only hinder our work. So if you have somewhere else to be, I suggest you leave." Her tone expressed finality.

"Then we'll hold you up no longer, inspector," replied Tania with as much dignity as she could muster, and she and Ron made their way out of the Town Hall and into the Market Square, just as a van drew up to disgorge several white-overall-clad individuals who hurried into the building.

*

"So what do you think?" asked Ron Faye across the table, as Dennis Dean, burley landlord of the Cross Keys, disappeared towards the hotel's kitchen bearing their order for the couple's somewhat delayed supper. "What happens next? What's the plan?"

"Another murder?" Tania screwed up her face. "Do I really want to get involved?"

71

"What's this 'I'?" smiled Ron. "I think you mean 'we', don't you? And as for getting involved, I don't see there's much of a choice. After all, it is your library ... well, in a manner of speaking. And Jenny's your friend, and you know several of the other people, so you're pretty well placed to sort out what's gone on. University academics don't just get murdered for no reason, do they?"

Tania sighed. "I suppose not. But you heard what Inspector Bright said. She's not going to take it too kindly if I go looking into something which she's told me, in no uncertain terms, is police business and none of my concern."

Ron adopted his most innocent expression. "But you won't be interfering in the work of the police, will you? You'll just be chatting to people about something which is going to cause a lot of talk around the town. Who could blame you for that?"

"You, Mr Faye," laughed Tania, "are a thoroughly devious person."

"I know. Great, isn't it?"

"And here's your food," announced Dennis Dean, as he arrived at the table bearing two laden plates. "Better late than never. So what was it that you had to rush off for in such a hurry, Ron?" he enquired. "You disappeared so fast that I never had a chance to ask."

"They've had a murder over at the Town Hall," replied Ron.

"Get away!" exclaimed Dennis. "Who? A local, was it?"

"Oh, probably nobody you would know," said Tania. "It was one of the members of the Literary Society. A professor from Camford. They were having a social function in the old library reading room over there, and while everyone was out of

72

the room having supper, he was killed. The police are over there now."

"Police!" snorted Dennis. "Who needs them when Ramston's got its very own Miss Marple in residence?"

"That's what I told her," grinned Ron.

"Anyway, I'll let you get on with your meals. But you know the whole town thinks I know everything that's going on, so I'll be needing full details."

"It's a promise." Ron picked up his knife and fork. "And this looks good, doesn't it, love?" He set to, appetite evidently in no way impaired by the recent encounter with a corpse.

"It does," agreed Tania. "And if you don't mind, no more talk of murder while we're eating."

Chapter 7

"You'll be wanting to talk to everyone who was there tonight, I imagine," said Ron, as the couple settled into bed. "Starting with Jenny, I suppose."

"I'll call her tomorrow," said Tania. "If I know her, she'll be bursting to tell me what happened after we left, and there's no way she'll be able to hold it in until next Saturday. And she won't be at work."

"Neither will you," pointed out Ron. "Good job you're closed on Sundays. Maybe that'll give you a chance to track down a couple of people while everything's fresh in their memories."

And so it was that, as soon as breakfast was finished, with Ron still at the sink attending to the washing up, Tania phoned Jenny's number.

"Oh Tania," gasped the dental nurse. "I was just going to call you. I've got so much to tell you."

"I thought you might have," responded Tania with a wry smile. "So when can we get together for a chat?"

"I can be at your place in ten minutes."

Tania laughed. "You'd better give Ron a chance to have his shower and get properly dressed. Why don't we make it an hour, and we'll have the coffee waiting."

To the second, the doorbell rang, and Ron ushered Jenny into the living room. "I'm so excited," she declared. "Now I know how you must feel, being involved with an actual murder case."

"I'm not actually involved," protested Tania. "I just don't like the thought of a violent death hanging over the place where I work."

"Well, I'll tell you one thing," said Jenny. "If you can solve the case before that Inspector Bright, I for one would be delighted. She was so rude to

74

everyone."

"That doesn't actually come as a great surprise," observed Ron. "So tell us, what went on after we'd left the premises?"

"You know we were all sent upstairs," began Jenny. "And then everyone had to sit down and give a statement to the sergeant, with the inspector hovering over his shoulder like a thundercloud. And they all said much the same thing – how they all went upstairs for supper, and when they came back down again, there was the professor, dead. I was left until last, for some reason, so I got to hear most of it. And some of it wasn't quite right, but I didn't like to butt in. I didn't want to get the rough edge of that woman's tongue."

"That's interesting," mused Tania.

"And there were a few things that I heard during the evening that I thought might be relevant, but again, having seen how that inspector spoke to you, I wasn't going to pipe up."

"Okay." Tania thought for a moment. "Right. Let's be methodical about this. For a start, who was where, and is there anyone we can rule out?"

"There's the boys who organised the murder evening, for a start," said Jenny. "They couldn't possibly have had anything to do with it."

"How so?"

"Because when we all came up for people to have their supper main course, they were with us, and so was the professor. But the boys took their supper and went down the back stairs to the kitchen to eat it – they said it didn't look right for the 'detectives' to mingle with the 'suspects'. And they were down there the whole time until Sam came up to say 'We're starting again', because the forty-five minutes were up"

"And where was the other one – Mike, was it?"

"Ah, now I discovered that he was changing into his costume for the next 'witness' in the mayor's private loo, just off the parlour."

"And there's no access to the reading room from the kitchen?"

"No," said Jenny. "That's why they couldn't serve the supper downstairs, according to the catering supervisor. Those back stairs only lead up to the mayor's parlour. And when all this was explained to Inspector Bright, she seemed satisfied, in her grumpy way."

"Right," nodded Tania. "So that's those two out of the reckoning. Good. Anyone else?"

"Alex and her friend. They were upstairs in the parlour the whole of supper time, because they were talking to me for some of it, and then I saw them sat in a corner together. I think they were comparing notes. Lindsey Doyle seemed to be taking the whole thing very seriously."

"And you're absolutely sure that they couldn't have left the parlour without you noticing?" Ron sought to confirm.

"Positive," stated Jenny. "I'd have noticed if Lindsey had gone anywhere, because to be honest, it was quite hard to keep my eyes off him. He's gorgeous. It's a shame he's not available. Not to me, anyway. Oh well," she sighed. "Some you win ..."

"So, moving on," resumed Tania, smiling. "That's two more off the table. Got any more?"

"Oh!" said Jenny. "I've just remembered. Annette was also upstairs the whole time."

"Annette Curtin, do you mean?" enquired Tania.

"Do you know her?" asked Ron.

Tania chuckled. "Oh yes. I should think everyone in Ramston knows her. Or if they don't, she knows all about them. She comes into the library a lot. She is absolutely the worst gossip in the whole of the town. If she doesn't know about it, it probably didn't happen. She makes Dennis Dean look like a rank amateur."

"She a patient at the surgery," added Jenny. "And she's always asking the other patients what's wrong with them, and how much their treatment costs. She's so nosy. Alison gets cross."

"And she didn't leave the parlour during the whole of the supper break?" asked Ron.

"No, because she was going about asking people if they had any ideas yet as to who did it, and what clues they'd picked up, just in case she'd missed something. In fact, she was so busy going about talking to people, or eavesdropping on their conversations, I'm surprised she had the chance to have anything to eat."

"That sounds," observed Ron, "as if she's a prime possible source of information. I bet Inspector Bright loved her."

"Oh no," disagreed Jenny. "The inspector didn't seem to have much time for her at all. When she heard she was upstairs at the crucial moment, she cut short all her twitterings and sent her off. I don't think Annette took that very well."

"Then she evidently needs a sympathetic ear," smiled Tania. "Which I'm sure I can provide."

"Two ears," put in Ron with a grin. "I suspect we'll be making a beeline for her quite soon. Do we have an address?"

"Of course," retorted Tania. "You married a librarian. We can do research, you know. Anyway, because she's one of the library's customers, I'll have her contact details on the library system."

"Is that actually a legitimate use of your position,

love?" enquired Ron, one eyebrow raised.

"Justified in pursuit of the greater good," riposted his wife. "Don't make waves."

"Sorry, love," grinned Ron.

"So, who's left?"

"Just the ones who were playing the 'suspects' in the game," replied Jenny.

"Well, that's neat, at least," said Ron. "Let's have a list, then. My pen is poised."

Jenny thought for a moment, and then counted them off on her fingers. "There's Roland Tighe the butcher, and Caroline Cash – she's the one with an antique shop just off the square. That weather girl from the television, Donna McIntosh, and there's a woman who does paintings – Monica de Glenn, her name is. Oh, and there's a lawyer called Jack Hughes, and a new member, Ivan Ocean. He's a student at Camford. And I think the last one was Ellen Dee. She's an electrician."

"That's a right mixed bunch," observed Ron. "Seven of them, by my count. And are they all based in Ramston?"

"All except that student boy," said Jenny. "He's at the university in Camford. Oh no, wait. I think he told Inspector Bright that the whole thing had knocked him sideways. So he was going to stay with his parents in Ramston for a few days."

"Very convenient," said Tania. "So, is that it for candidates?"

"I think so," said Jenny.

"In which case, I think you've earned your coffee after all that talking."

"Oh, there's more."

"Coffee first," insisted Tania. "And Ron, break out the digestives. And then when we've fortified ourselves, Jenny can spill a few more beans."

"The thing is," said Jenny, as Ron was pouring her second cup of coffee, "I thought things started to get a bit odd when Sam was doing the introduction to the evening, once everyone was sat around the table and ready to begin. He said 'Don't forget, everyone has a guilty secret'."

"He meant the characters in the game, right?" checked Tania.

"That's what he meant," nodded Jenny. "But there seemed to be a sudden change in atmosphere. Everyone froze for a moment."

"Everyone?" persisted Tania. "Or just our lucky seven?"

"Ooh, Tania, aren't you clever?" said Jenny. "Because I think you're right. It was just them."

"My wife is very intuitive, aren't you, love?" smiled Ron. "I can never get away with anything."

"So that was a moment when the atmosphere shifted?"

"I thought so at first," replied Jenny. "But then I realised, once I'd thought it through at home in the light of what happened later, that maybe I was wrong, and there was something in the wind earlier. You see, when people were first arriving, I was circulating with the tray of drinks, and as I was going round I could overhear odd little snippets of things people were saying to one another. And a lot of those involved the professor."

"Now that is exactly what we need," said Tania. "So what were these snippets?"

Jenny reflected for a moment. "I don't know what it was about Professor Kates," she began. "Did you know him, Tania?"

"No. I really haven't spent much time around the University of Camford, and I can't say that, after the

79

murder at the abbey, professors are really people that I'm happiest among. I know the name. And he was a professor of philosophy, I gather, and that's far too intellectual for the likes of me." She laughed.

"Don't do yourself down, love," said Ron. "Your intellect knocks spots off most people I know. Which I'm sure that other professor would have appreciated, if only he'd been alive to do so. And I'm sure this one would be the same, once you've solved the case. If he weren't dead."

"I think we may be getting ahead of ourselves," Tania pointed out. "We don't know a thing so far about what went on. So why don't we just let Jenny tell us? What was it you were going to say about Professor Kates, Jenny?"

"I was just going to say about his voice. It was quite odd – sort of low and raspy, but the thing was, it was quite penetrating. I mean, if you were near him, you could hear what he was saying to someone, even if you didn't mean to eavesdrop."

"Come on then," coaxed Ron. "Let's have some meat on the bones."

"It's funny you should say that," replied Jenny, "because one of the things I remember was when the professor was talking to Mr Tighe. We all know him, of course."

"Oh yes," nodded Tania. "He's quite a rarity. There aren't many independent butcher's shops left these days. Most of them have been put out of business by the supermarkets, so I always like to use Roland Tighe's shop as often as I can."

"His sausages are legendary," put in Ron. "Have you tried the pork and leek, Jenny?"

"We're not here to discuss menus, Ron," remarked Tania with some slight acerbity. "We're trying to winkle out some evidence."

"Wouldn't you need a fishmonger's for that?" grinned Ron.

"Ron!" Tania gave her husband a look, to which he responded with an expression of exaggerated innocence. "Do ignore the joker in the room, Jenny. He can't help himself sometimes. And please carry on with what you were saying."

"I'm not sure whether it was when we were all downstairs before the murder game started or whether it was upstairs during the first break," said Jenny. "I remember I was going around with a tray, but whether it was drinks or nibbles, I'm not quite sure. And I don't suppose it matters much anyway. The thing was, the professor was talking with Mr Tighe, and I was stood behind them giving something to someone, and I could hear what they were saying. And it wasn't anything to do with the university – he was going on about legal cases. Oh, that must have been it."

"What?"

"It must have been later, because the professor was playing a judge in the murder game. Lord Loverduck, I think he was. So it couldn't have been earlier, because people hadn't got their characters then."

"Hold on," said Ron. "That's not necessarily the case – no joke intended, love," he added, giving his wife a swift sidelong glance. "You know I always have a browse through the reports on court cases in the Ramston Evening Argus. I find it quite funny how many respectable members of the local great and good get had up for speeding. In fact, last year the mayor's official car was clocked doing eighty-five on the bypass."

"And this is relevant how?" asked Tania frostily.

"Sorry, love. It isn't really. But, the point is, these

things come up in the magistrates court. And guess what the name of one of the magistrates is."

Light dawned. "Professor Russell Kates, I assume," said Tania. "Which means that talk of cases could well be something that he'd encountered in that part of his life. So was it, Jenny?"

"Could have been. All I know is, the professor was saying that he'd been looking through the records of some old cases, for some reason, and he'd come across something which he found quite a surprise. Something involving a local shopkeeper's business during the war. And he said to Mr Tighe that he was going to dig deeper and try to put some meat on the bones. And Mr Tighe said that he didn't know what the professor meant, and that his was a very respectable family firm, but the professor said that from what he'd seen, there could be quite a bad smell about the whole thing. But then I looked round and Mr Tighe was walking off, and the professor was just standing there looking pleased with himself."

"Wonder what that was about?" mused Ron. "Maybe we'll have to pop into his shop for some of those sausages, love."

"Oh, that reminds me," said Jenny. "Talking of shops, there was that conversation I heard between the professor and the woman who runs that antique shop in town. You know – 'Carrie's Something-or-Other'."

"Caroline Cash, you mean?" said Tania. "Yes, I know her. I love going into that shop every so often, just to browse around. She's got some lovely things, and you never know what you're going to find. She's another one who comes into the library quite a lot, looking up maker's marks on ceramics or hallmarks on jewellery."

"And that was what she was talking to the professor about," declared Jenny. "Or rather, he was talking to her. And it was a bit odd, all about one of the clues on the evidence table."

Ron leaned forward, intrigued. "What, one of the weapons, do you mean?"

"No, funnily enough. It was a diamond necklace. Well, it was meant to be diamonds, but I don't suppose it was. It was said to have been stolen and then found in the home of one of the other characters."

"But in the game, obviously. And again, you definitely wouldn't risk using a genuine diamond necklace in that context," pointed out Tania. "So what made you think there was something odd about it?"

"The professor made some sort of joke about the stolen necklace being exactly the sort of thing that Carrie's character would be interested in, and maybe she might too, being in that line of business. And Carrie said that she wouldn't touch anything like that, because it would be too traceable. But then she stopped short and suddenly seemed to get flustered, and tried to say that wasn't what she meant, and the professor said that he'd be fascinated to find out more about her business, because there were all sorts of stories about dodgy items passing through antique shops, and maybe she'd like to tell him a few. But she said she didn't have time, and rushed off."

"Seems that Professor Kates had the knack of unsettling people, for some reason," observed Ron. "And I'm guessing that he unsettled somebody just a little too far, with unpleasant results."

"I think you're right," agreed Tania. "So maybe

Caroline's shop should also be on our itinerary. So, that's two of our seven where there seem to be some questions to be asked."

"Never two without three?" queried Ron. "Come on, Jenny – you must have somebody else."

"Well," said Jenny, "there was one more - that painter woman, Monica de Glenn. I did hear the professor talking to her right at the start of the evening, when people were arriving and everyone was still downstairs in the art gallery. But it didn't really seem to make any sense. I think the professor may have been making a joke, but I couldn't understand it."

"So what was this joke?" enquired Tania.

"He was stood in one of the alcoves looking at one of the paintings. One of the old masters that I think they're quite proud of. A Sizzler, or some such."

"Sisley, would that be?" suggested Ron. "Alfred Sisley. Nineteenth century Anglo-French Impressionist. Pretty valuable."

Jenny shrugged. "Maybe. Anyway, he called Miss de Glenn over and said he wanted her to have a look at it. He said he knew she had many creative talents, and he wanted her opinion. He knew Sisley's work well, he said. Especially the Catalogue of Raisins, or something like that." She pulled a face of bewilderment.

"*Catalogue Raisonné*, I think that must have been," explained Tania. "An official list of an artist's works."

"Oh," said Jenny, not sounding much the wiser. "Anyway, he said he knew there were so many fakes on the market, and some people were making a very fine living out of fine art. Some of it not so fine. And she said, how would she know, because she was just a humble portraitist. And he said,

84

surely not so humble, and where money was concerned it was often a case of oiling the wheels and then wielding the oils. 'Some of Sisley's works are impressive,' he said, 'but maybe some just leave a bad impression." And he laughed as if it was the greatest joke ever. And he turned on his heel and walked away, and just left her standing there."

Chapter 8

"That," said Ron, as he returned to the sitting room after seeing Jenny to the door, "was quite possibly very informative. It answered a few questions."

"And posed a whole lot more," replied Tania in a reflective tone.

Ron regarded his wife. "I know that look. You've got the bit between your teeth already, haven't you?"

"Does it show so much?" smiled Tania.

"You forget how well I know you, love," responded Ron. "You want to get on the hunt for the evil-doer straight away."

"While people's memories are still fresh," pointed out Tania. "Otherwise we could lose useful information."

"Good point. So, I've got my list. Why don't I also jot down the people that Jenny said could be ruled out because they never left the parlour, and then we can formulate a plan of campaign. Who do we talk to first?"

"Oh, I've already thought of that," replied Tania. "Alex Blaine. As secretary of the Literary Society, she was the principal organiser of the whole evening. Not only that, but she's a researcher. If there was anything to spot, I'm betting she'd be the most likely person to spot it."

"Sounds like a plan," nodded Ron. "Right. Let's get on the trail of our murderer."

*

Alexandra Blaine lived in a modest apartment in a former warehouse on the site of the old brewery in the heart of Ramston.

"I'm glad they found a way to re-use this place," remarked Ron as he pulled into a visitor space in the courtyard. He looked around admiringly at the cluster of red-brick buildings, most re-purposed from the original Victorian industrial structures, but with some new additions sympathetically designed to echo the atmosphere of the site. "It would have been so easy simply to demolish everything and put up a load of modern boxes. Probably cheaper too."

"I imagine the council would have had something to say on the subject if the developers had tried," responded Tania. "They're pretty hot on preserving the character of the town. And I'd have been one of the first to start waving protest placards if anyone had attempted to do anything of the kind."

"Good job it wasn't necessary. So, where is it that Alex lives?"

Tania frowned in concentration. "Flat 7 in The Maltings, if I remember correctly. Which is ..." She scanned the surrounding buildings. "... that one over there."

"How do you know these things?" wondered Ron. "I wasn't aware that you and Alex were close chums."

"We aren't. But researchers do use libraries, you know. And librarians have strange and mysterious skills when it comes to finding out things, like addresses. It's not that difficult, actually. Ever heard of the electoral roll?" Tania led the way to the entrance of the block in question and pressed a button on the keypad.

"Hello."

"Hello. Is that Alex?"

"Yes." The voice held a note of wariness.

"It's Tania Faye from the library. I'm here with my husband Ron. Sorry to bother you on a Sunday, but I wondered if we could have a chat about what happened last night."

A pause. *"Oh. All right. Second floor."*

There was a buzz, and Tania pushed open the door into the lobby.

The face that greeted Tania and Ron at the door of Alex's flat was pale, with dark circles under the eyes. Alex stepped back and gestured her visitors into the living room, modern and open-plan with a kitchen at one end and large windows overlooking the rooftops of Ramston at the other. She indicated an oversized squashy sofa for the couple, and sank into an armchair, seeming to hunch up as she wordlessly wrapped her arms around a cushion.

Tania immediately had the feeling that Alex was not coping at all well with the situation. "How are you?" she asked tentatively.

The question seemed to trigger an immediate release of emotion in Alex. "Oh, it's just awful," she gasped, blinking back tears. "I've never been involved with anything like this before. I mean, I've had to research murder stories for my job in the past, but that's always been at arm's length. It's not the same. I've never even seen an ... an actual body before. And I just keep seeing pictures in my mind of the professor lying there with his head all twisted ..." She took a deep shuddering breath and attempted a wan half-smile. "As you can probably guess, I didn't get a lot of sleep last night."

"I can imagine," sympathised Tania. "Are you sure you don't mind talking about it now?"

"It might help," added Ron. "You know, exorcise the demons. And Tania does feel an odd sort of responsibility, things having taken place in her library, so to speak. She really would like to help find out what happened."

Alex took another breath and seemed to reach a resolution. She sat up. "You're probably right." She wiped her eyes with the back of her hand. "So, what do you want to know?" Another half-smile. "Although it feels a bit odd to be on the receiving end. I'm usually the one asking the questions."

"When I first got there," began Tania, "everyone seemed to be standing around at something of a loss, but then the police arrived. And once Inspector Bright had seen what the situation was, I remember your friend suggested to her that you would be the best person to explain what had happened so far. Which, as far as I remember, you did very clearly. But then the inspector more or less told Ron and me that we weren't wanted, so we left. So what happened after that?"

"We were all sent back upstairs," said Alex, "and then everyone had to sit down with the inspector and give a statement. Not that I could tell her very much more than I'd already said. But then all of a sudden it hit me. Somebody from our society had actually been murdered, and it had to have been one of us. One of my friends. And that was when I started to get upset. And Lindsey – that's the friend I was there with – he asked the inspector if he could give his statement straight away so that he could bring me home. Not that she was too pleased about that. I don't think she likes being told what to do. But she said all right, and since Lindsey was with me pretty much the whole time, there wasn't really anything different he could tell her, so once he'd finished, we left. And he brought me back here. He said he'd stay if I wanted, but I told him I'd be fine, so he went home." A tear began to emerge.

"But obviously, fine is the one thing I wasn't."

"I know it's not easy," said Tania. "Ron and I discovered a body once, and it gives you a pretty big jolt. However," she smiled, "there is one sovereign remedy for that. A nice cup of tea."

"Oh, I'm so sorry." Alex started to struggle to her feet. "I didn't even think ..."

"No, you stay right where you are," commanded Tania briskly. "If there's one thing Ron is very good at, it's making tea. Ron, I'm sure you can find your way around Alex's kitchen ..."

"I'm on it." Ron bounded to his feet and made a beeline for the kettle.

"... and you and I can carry on with our chat. Because what interests me most is what went on before you all came downstairs together from the mayor's parlour and found Professor Kates."

"Actually ..." Alex furrowed her brow. "Actually, we didn't *all* come down together at all."

"Ah!" Tania leaned forward intently. "Now that's what I was getting at. According to my colleague Jenny, some people stayed upstairs all the time during the main course break, but some others were absent at various times. I think I remember you telling Inspector Bright something of the sort. The question is, who was absent and when? So what can you remember?"

Alex's face was a picture of concentration. "Actually, I think the professor was the first to go back downstairs. More or less straight away."

Tania's eyebrows rose in surprise. "Really? You mean he didn't have any main course at all?"

"No, he didn't. Because I was right next to him when we got to the table where the buffet was laid out, and he took one look and grunted something about hating quiche. And I felt a bit responsible, having been the one who made all the arrangements, and I said that we could probably organise something as an alternative – goodness knows what – but he said he was going back downstairs anyway because there was something he wanted to take a closer look at."

"What, something to do with the murder mystery, you mean?"

"He didn't say," said Alex. "But I suppose it must have been."

"There was that table down in the art gallery with all the so-called evidence items on it," intervened Ron, placing a tray with mugs of tea and a jug of milk on the coffee table. "Maybe he wanted to steal a march on the others in solving the mystery. And," he added with meaningful emphasis, "among all the bits and pieces was that antique police truncheon. And if I'm any good at picking up vibes, I wouldn't mind betting that that is what Inspector Bright has short-listed as being the actual murder weapon that the professor was attacked with."

"Yes, but he couldn't have known in advance that he would be on the receiving end of it," objected Tania. "If that's what he was. It could have been anything. And I don't see how the evidence items could be relevant anyway, because they were all brought in by Sam and Mike as part of the story. What were they, anyway?"

Alex shook her head. "I can only remember a couple. There was ..."

"Hold on," interrupted Ron. "We all saw that table. So this may be where my boy scout training kicks in."

"Your what?" laughed Tania. "What has you having been a boy scout in your youth got to do with anything?" She turned to Alex. "I've seen

91

pictures of Ron in his khaki shorts. All kneecaps and elbows. But I don't see how this is relevant to what we're talking about."

"Patience, sceptical one," retorted Ron. "We didn't just go about learning knots and getting stones out of horses' hooves, you know. There were practical benefits, among them observation and memory training."

"Go on," said Tania, intrigued.

"There was a thing called Kim's Game," explained Ron. "It's just the sort of parlour game the Victorians used to play. You had a tray of objects, all different, which you studied for a few minutes, and then the tray was covered with a cloth, and you had to remember as many of the items as you could. Brain training, you see. And as it happens, I was rather good at it."

"And you think you can remember all the items on that evidence table, even though we only saw it briefly?" Tania sounded doubtful.

"I'll give it a go." Ron closed his eyes. "Right. For a start, there was the truncheon. That's the easy bit. Plus there were a couple of other things that were obviously candidates as murder weapons. I remember there was a dagger ... there was a bottle of poison ... oh, and a syringe next to it. Useful for injecting the victim, but not this time around, obviously. Um ... there were quite a few sheets of typescript ..."

"Those would have been the witness statements from the mystery," murmured Alex to Tania. "but that was all made-up stuff. Surely that's not what we're looking for."

"Ah!" exclaimed Ron, eyes still shut. "There was a scrawled note – well, half of one. Red ink on blue paper. It had been torn." His eyes could be seen scanning the scene behind his closed eyelids. "There were a couple of valuable items too … a silver hip-flask, and that necklace which Jenny mentioned – the one which was genuine fake diamonds. I think that's about it. Oh no, hang on. One more thing. There was a rubber glove. A yellow one." He opened his eyes, blinking at the brightness.

"That's brilliant, Ron," said Alex. "I don't know how you do that. It sounds like the notes our continuity girls make when they're shooting a drama. And as far as I can tell, you only got one thing wrong."

"That being …" Ron was curious.

"The last one. The glove. Except that it wasn't just one. It was a pair."

"Are you sure?"

"Absolutely. Because Willy Evertwigg told us that the pair of gloves was used by the housekeeper when opening Lord Loverduck's safe to steal the necklace."

"Just a second." Ron closed his eyes once more in recollection. "Well, there might have been a pair when Willy Whatsit was going on about them, but there was only one on that table when we saw it. I'm positive. I'd swear to it if I had to."

"And if that's right …" Tania's voice held suppressed excitement. "That would mean that whoever used the truncheon on the professor picked it up using the rubber glove so that it wouldn't have their fingerprints on it. Just like the fictitious housekeeper."

"But then why didn't they just put the glove back with the truncheon afterwards?" wondered Alex. "In case its absence was noticed?"

"And nobody did notice until Ron did his very

clever memory trick," pointed out Tania. "Which goes to show how unobservant most people are. And I'm guessing that our murderer was actually quite cunning not to replace the glove, because if it were identified as having been used in the murder, the interior would have traces of the wearer's DNA. Crucial evidence. No, that glove was either concealed at the scene or removed ..."

"... and if nobody left the scene after the body was discovered," jumped in Ron, "it couldn't have been removed. It's still there somewhere. And somebody is going to have to go back to retrieve it."

"Which brings us back to the matter of who left the mayor's parlour during that crucial forty-five minutes," said Tania. "Alex, can you recall anyone's movements? You told Inspector Bright that some people went to the loo, and someone went outside for a cigarette. Can you remember in any more detail?"

"Ivan!" suddenly exclaimed Alex. "He went to light up in the parlour. He'd been twitchy all evening – I don't think he was enjoying himself. But Caroline Cash jumped on him and stopped him, and said she'd take him out to the smoking shelter just outside by the Town Hall steps, because she could do with a cigarette herself. That must have been about quarter past nine or so. I didn't see when they came back – I was talking to Lindsey most of the time."

"Perhaps he will have noticed," said Tania. "Anyone else?

"Not that I can think of," replied Alex.

"And what about Professor Kates himself? You say he spoke to you before he went off pretty soon after you'd all broken for refreshments. Did you speak to him earlier in the evening?"

"No, but actually, I did overhear him speaking to Ivan earlier on. Maybe that was part of the reason Ivan was jumpy. I can understand it, I suppose – student and professor and so on. It's bound to be a bit intimidating."

"So what was said?"

"I didn't really hear much. It seemed to be something to do with student matters anyway. The professor said he'd been asked to look into the finances of the Students' Union at Camford, which he knew Ivan had a lot to do with, and he said something about interesting revelations. Maybe he wanted Ivan to help him explain some of the queries he had. But that was it."

"Any other conversations of any interest?" enquired Tania. "Not that I'm suggesting you went around eavesdropping all evening, of course. But Jenny did mention that the professor's voice was quite penetrating, so you probably couldn't help hearing him."

"You're right, actually," smiled Alex. "And I think it must have been during the first break, when most of us were gathered around the evidence table to see the latest additions. And the professor was next to Jack Hughes who was looking through the witness statements, and he made some remark about the statements not having been particularly well written. And he said he always appreciated a well-written piece of work. As did some of his judicial colleagues. And Jack said he didn't know what he meant, and the professor said that so many statements were pure fiction, but it was the impure fiction that could lead to trouble. He said that he happened to know a highly-placed customer for a particular style of fiction, and that people in such positions could easily be coerced into arranging career advancement in exchange for discretion. And Jack said that he had no idea what the professor was talking about, and he went off to get a drink. He looked as if he needed it."

"Intriguing," remarked Tania. "I wonder what all that was about. I hope the professor didn't spend the whole evening going around making oblique remarks to the others."

"Oh, not at all," replied Alex. "In fact, he was very complimentary to one of the members."

"Who was that?"

"Monica de Glenn, the painter. It was in the art gallery early on. She was standing by some painting or other – I can't remember which – and the professor said that he'd heard great things about her skills. He told her that he'd done a fine arts course when he was a student, many years ago, and that he'd made a close study of the styles of several of the impressionist painters. And he said something about her having a remarkable talent."

"And what did she say to that?"

"Well, nothing, really. She seemed at something of a loss as to how to reply. Embarrassed, probably. But then someone came over to talk to me, so I didn't hear any more."

Chapter 9

"I'm not sure who we ought to talk to next," said Tania as the couple returned to the car. "Maybe Jack Hughes. I have an idea he lives around here somewhere."

"Maybe nobody," retorted Ron firmly. "Have you seen the time? If an army marches on its stomach, I'm pretty sure that an amateur detective force does too. And Sunday lunch is a sacred British tradition which I, for one, am not prepared to forgo. So, home first, and you can do some armchair sleuthing while I'm occupied in the kitchen."

"You're the chef," smiled Tania. "Home it is."

*

"I'll tell you what we need," said Tania, as the pair entered the sitting room. "A timeline."

"What, you mean a schedule of who was where and when? Good idea, love," agreed Ron. "Shame we didn't get one from Jenny."

"Blast! Why didn't I think of that? I'd better give her a call."

"Aha!" grinned Ron. "No need, actually."

"Why not?" Tania looked puzzled.

"Time for the great detective to employ her little grey cells," replied Ron. "We can use our forensic skills to establish times."

"I have no idea what you're talking about."

Ron reached for his phone. "It's all here." He began to tap the screen. "Think about it. You sent me a text to say that you were just finishing up in the library, and that you'd be over to the Cross Keys in a couple of minutes."

"So ...?"

"And just afterwards, when you hadn't appeared,

I phoned you to check where you were. So that's it! Here." He held out the phone for Tania to see. "Thank goodness for smartphones. There's your text, timed at 21.42." More taps. "And there's my call to you, timed at 21.47, and that was when you told me that they'd found a body. So put those together, and allowing for Jenny's frantic sprint to find you after the professor's body had been discovered, and we can put the time of the discovery pretty accurately at quarter to ten, or as near as makes no difference."

"Well done you," smiled Tania appreciatively. "I knew my Watson had hidden reserves of brilliance."

"I have my uses," responded Ron. "But there's more. If you remember, Jenny said that Sam, or Inspector Evertwigg, or whoever he was at that moment, came to her in the mayor's parlour to say that they were just about to recommence, as the forty-five minutes allowance for main courses was up."

"So she did," recalled Tania.

"Which means," continued Ron, "that as the company was invited to reassemble at nine forty-five, they had broken for refreshments at nine o'clock. So there, love," he finished triumphantly, "is your window of opportunity!"

Tania deposited a kiss on Ron's cheek. "You, darling, are brilliant. So all we need to do is establish who last saw the professor, and which of the seven deadly suspects was absent from the mayor's parlour and when, and what their devious motives may be, and there's our solution." She gave a small grunt of resignation. "It's going to be fun trying to figure that lot out."

"What, with all those people to talk to, and your

subtle inquisitorial skills encouraging them to drop incriminating information left, right, and centre?" laughed Ron. "Piece of cake."

"I admire your optimism." Tania gave a rueful smile.

"And on the subject of food," said Ron, getting to his feet, "Sunday lunch isn't going to cook itself. So I shall disappear into the kitchen and attempt to do something imaginative with a couple of pork chops, and then we can formulate a plan of campaign. Who do we talk to next?"

*

"Don't think I didn't notice you slaving away over a hot laptop while I was doing the same over a hot stove," grinned Ron, as the couple sat back sipping coffee after lunch. "So what conclusions has my favourite sleuth come to? Who's your next target for grilling?"

"You make it sound so intimidating," protested Tania. "I can't grill anybody. I'd like to see Inspector Bright's face if she caught me doing anything of the kind. All I'm doing is having a friendly chat and lending a sympathetic ear to people who've been caught up in an unpleasant situation."

"Yes, dear," replied Ron with a broad smile, muttering under his breath, "And I'm Queen Marie of Romania."

Tania affected not to hear the remark. "And while you were elsewhere, I thought I'd put the time to good use by working out the best time and place to get in touch with our list of interested parties."

"Using your friend the electoral roll as a source again?" queried Ron.

"All-sorts," said Tania. "Anyway, I thought the first person we ought to speak to would be Ivan

Ocean."

"But he's a student at Camford, isn't he?

"He is. Third year Politics, Philosophy and Economics, to be exact."

"Gosh, you have been doing your homework. But surely you don't want to schlep all the way over to Camford?"

"No need. Don't you remember, Jenny told us that he was planning on staying with his parents in Ramston for a few days because of the shock of events. But we can't be sure how long he'll be around. Maybe the lure of Academe will draw him back to Camford sooner rather than later, so I'd rather get to him today. And I've got his parents' address, and while you were clattering about in the kitchen I took the precaution of calling his mother, who seems a lovely woman, and has asked us round for a cup of tea at five o'clock."

"You amaze me," said Ron, depositing a kiss on the tip of his wife's nose. "That means there's time for a siesta before we hit the trail again."

*

Ivan Ocean's family home was an unremarkable 1930s three-bedroomed semi-detached house of the type found in so many suburbs throughout the country, with a neat front garden featuring a small lawn surrounded by flower-filled borders, and net curtains at all the windows. On the drive, a slightly-battered Fiat hatchback was drawn up behind a middle-aged but gleamingly-maintained Vauxhall saloon. Tania rang the doorbell, and smiled quietly at the sound of the Westminster chimes echoing faintly in the hall of the house.

Ivan's mother turned out to be a smiling dumpling of a woman with greying hair, wearing a cardigan over a print dress. "Come in, come in," she

100

said, stepping back and gesturing her visitors into the front room. "I'm Margery, Ivan's mother. And you're Tania, aren't you? I didn't realise when we spoke, but I recognise you from when I've been into the library."

"And this is my husband Ron," replied Tania. "It's very kind of you to see us."

"Well, how could I not?" replied Margery. "After the shock our poor Ivan's had. He told us all about it when he turned up on our doorstep last night. I couldn't believe it. What a dreadful thing to happen, and in your library too. I can see why you're upset about it."

"Well, that's the thing," said Tania, smoothly picking up her cue. "I think everyone's upset by the situation, and my thought was that it might make things better if we can talk about it, rather than keeping everything bottled up."

"I couldn't agree more," said Margery. She looked around and lowered her voice. "Not like my Reg. That's my husband. He's up the shed now. Says he doesn't want to talk about it." She sighed. "Well, we all have different ways of coping."

"So where's Ivan now?" enquired Ron.

"Oh, he's out in the conservatory. I thought it would be better for him to talk to you there. He won't want me fussing around. You know, 'Oh mum!', that sort of thing. So if you'd like to go through, and I'll bring your tea out to you."

Ivan turned from gazing out of the window as the visitors joined him in the conservatory. He was taller than Tania recalled from the previous evening, with a mop of dark fringe falling over his face and a gangly frame which he didn't seem to have quite grown into. "I remember you from last night," he said. "Mum said you wanted to talk." He

101

frowned. "But I thought I'd told the police everything when they were taking statements. I don't know what more I can say."

"We're not actually connected with the police," replied Tania. "But because I'm in charge of the town's library where the murder ..." Ivan flinched. "Sorry ... where it happened, I feel some odd sort of responsibility, and I need to find out how things were. So, do you mind if we sit down?"

Ivan shrugged. "Help yourself." He slumped into a rattan armchair, while Tania and Ron took a seat side-by-side on the accompanying sofa.

"Can I just ask how come you were at the murder mystery evening in the first place?" wondered Ron. "No offence, but you don't exactly seem the type to be attracted by either whodunnits or the finer aspects of literary appreciation."

"It's my tutor at Uni," replied Ivan. "He suggested it. Said that there were things about my writing style that ought to be sharpened up. He reckoned that joining a literary society would help. And I couldn't really say no, not with my dissertation coming up. He has a say in assessing it. And he had a contact at Ramston, so he pointed me in that direction."

"And who could possibly have guessed how events would have turned out?" Ron shook his head sorrowfully.

"Here's your tea," announced Margery Ocean brightly, as she bustled in from the direction of the kitchen, bearing a tray. "Now, who takes milk?"

"Oh, just leave it there and we can help ourselves," said Ron and, as Margery disappeared with a backward look of concern towards her son, he turned to his wife in invitation for her to continue.

"I gather from your mother that you were quite affected by what happened at the Town Hall last night," began Tania, as Ron poured.

Ivan frowned. "Did she say that?" Another shrug. "Maybe. It's not every day you get somebody murdered a few yards away from you."

"But I understood that being upset by the murder was one of the reasons you didn't go back to Camford last night," said Tania. "Didn't someone hear you say that? Which was why you decided to come back here to stay with your parents."

"Oh, that. Well, maybe I did say that, but really, it was so's I could get out from under the police with all their questions. And I might have had a couple of drinks, and I couldn't be bothered to drive back to the Uni. This was the easy option. And I knew Mum would flap when she heard anyway, so it saved me the trouble of having to tell her all about it today."

"I see." The young man's attitude puzzled Tania slightly. "But I imagine that the professor's death must nevertheless have come as some kind of a shock to you. I'm guessing you must have been reasonably close to him at Camford."

Ivan shook his head. "Not specially, no."

"Oh. You surprise me. You're doing a PPE degree, aren't you? And I believe Professor Kates was a philosophy professor."

"They have more than one. Camford's a big university." Ivan sounded defensive.

"Of course," returned Tania smoothly. "So he wasn't particularly known to you before the events of last night? Your paths hadn't crossed."

"Like I said."

"It's just that someone told me that they'd heard the professor speaking to you at some point in the evening. Something about the Student Union, I think they said. Finance, or some such?"

Tania thought she detected a flash of unease in Ivan's eyes. "What about it?" he asked.

"Can you remember why Professor Kates might have expressed an interest in the subject?"

There was a pause, before Ivan's frown cleared and was replaced by a bright and confident-looking smile. "Oh, right. I remember now. It must have been about the grant we're getting."

"A grant? Sounds interesting." Tania sipped her tea.

Ivan was sounding more relaxed now. "Yes. There's been a rumour about some big donor making a grant towards the refurbishment of the Union building. It needs it. It's a bit shabby these days. That must have been it."

"And the Union hasn't funds of its own?" queried Tania. "From what I've heard, these institutions are usually rolling in it."

"Well, not us," said Ivan shortly. He seemed unwilling to expand.

"And that must have been the 'interesting revelations' that the professor was heard to speak about," smiled Tania blandly. "Well, that obviously clears that up. So was that the only time you had words with the professor during the course of the evening?"

"Words?" Ivan shifted uneasily.

"Yes. I mean, did you and he speak after that? Other than during the course of the murder mystery game. You see, I'm trying to get a picture of who spoke to whom and when. Particularly during the time when people were upstairs in the mayor's parlour for their supper main course. Did you see the professor speaking to anyone else at that time?"

"No. In fact, he didn't stay long up there at all." Ivan sounded on firmer ground. "I saw him go back downstairs pretty soon after we all went up. No idea why. And then after I'd had something to eat, I went outside for a ciggy."

"Alone?"

"No. That Caroline woman, the one with the antique shop, came too. She showed me where the smoking shelter was. But she finished before me, and she went back inside."

"So you were left on your own. Do you have any idea where she went?"

"Not a clue." A slight smile. "Actually, that's quite funny. Because she said something about not having a clue, so she needed to check up on something. I didn't really listen. But after I finished I just sat there for a while, and then I went back upstairs. I wanted another drink."

"And you didn't see Caroline or the professor when you went back inside?"

"Sorry, no. Can't help you."

"You didn't go back into the reading room?"

"Why would I?"

"Or see anyone else who did?"

"What, like some mad-eyed maniac waving that truncheon about? You don't suppose I might have mentioned the fact to the coppers?"

Tania chose to ignore the sarcastic tone in Ivan's voice. "And you didn't see or hear anything during the course of the early evening that might make you think that there was some kind of conflict or situation between Professor Kates and any of the other people who were there? No harsh words overheard?"

Ivan shook his head. "Nothing. And why am I

getting all these questions anyway? You said you were nothing to do with the police, and I've already given them a statement. If you want to know anything, why don't you ask them?"

"Maybe we will," said Tania, getting to her feet. "Well, we'd better not take up any more of your time. Please thank your mother for the tea." She and Ron made their way out to the front door, which closed behind them to the sound of a slightly-surprised 'Oh! Bye!' from the direction of the kitchen.

*

"And what did you make of that then?" asked Ron, as he pulled away from the kerb.

"I'll say one thing for Ivan," replied Tania. "He's a pretty good bluffer."

"You didn't buy that Student Union grant story then?"

"Not for a second," declared Tania. "And if there was an award for unconvincing smiles, the one that Ivan produced at that moment would get my vote. So the question then becomes, what were these 'interesting revelations' that Jenny heard spoken of?"

"Sadly, Professor Kates isn't in any position to pass those on to us. And unless your brilliant researching techniques can run something to earth, we may never know."

"I'll give that some thought," mused Tania. "If there's some sort of a motive there, maybe it's somewhere out there."

"One thing struck me," observed Ron. "That mention of the maniac with the truncheon. You don't suppose Ivan was giving himself away, do you?"

Tania shook her head. "I don't think so. It seemed

106

pretty clear that Inspector Bright fastened on to the truncheon the moment she saw it, so it wasn't anything that nobody knew. It would be too much to hope for that Ivan was blurting out his guilty secret."

"Unless it was a crafty double-bluff on his part. Ho hum. Just kicking ideas around."

"I suspect we'll be doing plenty of that before we're finished," smiled Tania wryly.

"But not, I think, tonight," said Ron with sudden decisiveness. "I reckon we, and by that I mean chiefly you, have done enough pate-cudgelling for one day. The professor's not been dead for twenty-four hours yet, so it's early days, and I suspect there's plenty more to find out before we've finished. So what I suggest is that, once we get in, you go and have one of your nice longs baths while I rustle up a bit of supper, and then we can settle down in front of the television with a large glass of wine and watch a sloppy old black-and-white movie. With absolutely no murders in it."

Tania leaned across the car to rest her head momentarily on her husband's shoulder. "You, darling, are good to me. What did I do to deserve you?"

"Oh, I'm sure you'll find some way to thank me," said Ron airily. "We could always have an early night." The words were accompanied by a roguish grin.

Tania raised one eyebrow. "Maybe," she replied, with an echoing quiet smile.

*

"You're ready early," remarked Ron. "We don't need to leave for ages yet."

"I thought I'd walk to work this morning," replied Tania. "Save you the bother of running me in. And

I'm sure you must have work you can be getting on with at home. You can't go neglecting your clients just because Ramston's got another murder on its hands."

"It would give me a chance to finish that work I started on Saturday night," admitted Ron. "If you're sure."

"It's a beautiful morning," said Tania firmly. "The walk will do me good. Fresh air, and maybe some fresh thoughts. I can chew over who we need to talk to next."

"In which case, how about I come into town and meet you for lunch?" suggested Ron. "You can share your dazzling new thinking with me."

"Deal," smiled Tania, and picked up her handbag.

Chapter 10

Despite her words, Tania found that no thoughts of the murder intruded on her journey to work. She simply enjoyed the clear air and the blue sky, the dappled shade shed by the full foliage of the horse-chestnut trees along The Avenue, and the twitterings of the unseen birds hiding amongst their leaves, and almost without her realising it, her feet had directed themselves to the Market Square. She had scarcely had time to unlock the library front door, greet her weekday assistant and set her to work re-shelving the weekend's returned volumes, and settle herself behind her desk with thoughts of the day's tasks ahead, when a familiar voice broke her concentration.

"Tania. Isn't all this a dreadful business."

Tania looked up to see the excited features of Annette Curtin looking across the counter at her. "Oh, good morning, Miss Curtin," she greeted the first customer of the day. "I'm sorry, I didn't notice you. I must have been miles away."

"Thinking about this awful murder, I expect," replied Annette in sepulchral tones. "I don't blame you."

"No, actually I was about to check whether there were any updates on our system software," protested Tania.

"Oh no, I wouldn't blame you at all," continued Annette, blithely ignoring Tania's reply. "I know I haven't been able to think of anything else since Saturday. And I've hardly had a wink of sleep. I'm sure I must look ghastly." Annette's shiny face and bright eyes cast doubt on her words.

"Not a bit of it," said Tania cheerfully. "You look absolutely fine to me. So, what can I do for you?"

She looked the other woman up and down. "You don't look as if you're returning anything today. So is there anything in particular you're after?"

"Oh. Um ... yes." Annette seemed thrown off her stride by Tania's robust responses. "Yes, actually, there is. I was wondering if you had . .. um ..."

"Yes?" Tania hid a smile. Annette was obviously having to do some swift improvising.

"Yes, that's it! A book about Richard III. How they found his grave. You see, there was a programme on television, and I wondered ..."

"I don't believe we have anything on the shelves at the moment, but let me check and I'll see what I can do," said Tania. "Just leave it with me. Was there anything else?"

Annette was evidently determined not to be thwarted in her intention to bring up the subject of the death of Russell Kates. "Such a sad and sudden death, the poor king," she declared. "Just like the professor, in a way. And I don't suppose you've heard anything? You know, whether the police are any further forward?"

Tania shook her head. "Nothing, I'm afraid. But then, there isn't any reason why I should. The police don't share their information with me. After all, I'm just a librarian." She gave her most innocent smile.

"Of course, you've seen that policeman standing guard outside the Town Hall front entrance," ploughed on Annette.

"Actually, no," said Tania. "I didn't notice anyone when I arrived."

"Perhaps he was inside. Examining the scene of the crime. I just happened to pop into the front hall, merely to take a look, of course, and they had festoons of that black-and-yellow tape they use

110

across the entrance to the Art Gallery, so nobody could go in."

"Oh, what a shame," responded Tania, her sympathetic reply as genuine-sounding as she could make it.

"I just wondered if I could help in any way. After all, it's the duty of every honest citizen to assist the police at times like this."

"But I'm sure you've already done that, haven't you?" queried Tania. "Surely you'll have given a statement on Saturday night. I know Inspector Bright was certainly intending to get statements from everyone present."

"Hmmm. That Inspector Bright," harrumphed Annette. "I really don't know how good she is at her job. She doesn't seem like a proper detective at all."

"How do you mean?" asked Tania, intrigued.

"Well, she wanted to know who was where at what point in the evening. And of course, though I say it as shouldn't, I'm quite an observant person."

Tania bit her lip. "I think I may have heard that said about you. Such a useful talent, I should imagine." She couldn't help a small snort of mirth escaping.

"But when I told her that I hadn't left the mayor's parlour during the period when we were supposed to be having our supper main course," sailed on Annette blithely, "she was most dismissive. Told me that, since it was unlikely that I would be able to contribute any further useful information, I could go. I was really quite offended."

"You would be. I can see that." Tania was managing to maintain an admirably straight face.

"So of course, I never got to tell her anything about all the other things I knew. Well, that's her loss." Annette's lips were pinched together.

Tania's attention was alerted. "Other things?" she enquired casually.

"Oh yes. Everybody talks, you know. And mostly they don't care whether they're heard or not. Mind you, I dare say most people don't pay the slightest attention to what's going on around them. Not observant, you see."

"Whereas you are, of course."

"As you say." Annette preened.

Tania looked around the library. So far there had been no further visitors, and her assistant was still busily occupied with the trolley of returns at the far end. "So you're saying that there were things said on Saturday night which you think may have some bearing on what happened to the professor?"

"Well, I really couldn't say for certain. And as I'm sure you realise, I'd be the last person to eavesdrop deliberately on anyone, or to gossip about things that don't concern me."

"Naturally." Tania nodded solemnly. "But the thing is, sometimes one simply can't help hearing what other people say. It's not intentional. It just happens. Especially if a certain person chances to have a loud or piercing voice."

"That's just it!" declared Annette. "And if there's one person who had a loud voice on Saturday, it was that professor. I got the impression that he thought a great deal of himself. Probably because he was some sort of academic high-up, or so they said. I should think he had the habit of looking down on other people."

"Can you think of any of the people he might have been looking down on, by any chance?"

Annette thought for a moment. "The young ones, mostly. Like that girl who works for the television, for instance."

"What, Alex Blaine? The secretary of the Literary Society?"

"No, not her. The other one. The pretty one. The one who does the weather."

"Oh, Donna McIntosh. Yes, she's quite a new member of the Society, didn't I hear?"

Annette nodded. "She is, but it wasn't the Society that the professor was speaking to her about. It was something to do with her job."

"I wonder why a philosophy professor at Camford University would be interested in Donna's job. You wouldn't have thought the two things would have much in common," mused Tania.

"You wouldn't, would you," agreed Annette. "I thought it sounded rather strange myself. I suppose that's what caught my attention. Just as I happened to be passing, of course."

"And this was where and when?"

"Sometime early in the evening, I think." It was clear to Tania that Annette could remember exactly, despite her attempt at casualness. "Yes, it must have been in the Art Gallery while people were arriving, before the event got going properly. I remember, Alex was going around chatting to people with her secretarial hat on, because some of us weren't quite sure what was happening and she wanted to encourage the social side of the event, and I think Donna was standing on her own looking a little bit lost, and the professor was nearby, and Alex said that Donna as a new member must have a chat with the professor, because he was patron of the Society and he could tell her a lot about what went on, so she introduced them, and said what Donna did, and the professor said something like 'Oh yes, I think I may have heard of

113

you'. So Donna did a sort of blushing smile and said she got that a lot, and lots of her fans said nice things to her, and the professor said that unfortunately, what he'd heard wasn't necessarily something that Donna ought to be pleased about. And she blinked a bit and said she didn't know what he meant, and he told her that he was an old friend of one of the directors of the television station, and from what he'd heard, the TV company had some very interesting promotional processes. He said it wasn't always who you knew or what you knew, but what you did and for who. And Donna went quite pale and stuttered a bit, but then that girl with the drinks came up and the professor turned to take one, and by the time he'd turned back, Donna had vanished."

"And what did you make of that?" wondered Tania.

"I'm sure I couldn't say," said Annette. She pursed her lips. "He was a very much older man, and she's a young girl. Make of that what you will. And she wasn't the only young girl I heard him speaking to."

"How do you mean?"

"I say young girl," said Annette. "I mean, she's not quite as young as that Donna girl, but she's still quite a lot younger than the professor."

"And this would be ...?"

"Ellen Dee. Do you know her? The electrician. Nice girl. She came round to do some work for one of my neighbours. I was dusting my windowsill, and quite by chance I just happened to see her van outside. Now she's one of the Society's members who has absolutely no pretensions as a writer. Unlike some of them, who fancy their talents." A sniff. "Mostly with no good reason at all. Now there's one man ..."

"You were talking about Ellen Dee," broke in Tania.

"Yes, that's right. She comes to the meetings because she loves to read, she says. Actually, she makes some quite clever contributions when we're discussing a particular book we've been reading around. She's quite a bright girl." Annette gave an unexpected little giggle. "I suppose she would be, being an electrician."

"And you say that you heard some sort of exchange between her and Professor Kates?" said Tania, attempting to bring Annette back on track.

"I did," nodded Annette. "And I know when that was, because we'd gone up to the mayor's parlour during the first break in the murder game, and I'd got my little plate of canapés and was coming away from the table, and I was passing behind the professor when he stepped back and trod right on my foot. He'd obviously not noticed me, but he didn't make the slightest attempt to apologise, and I was about to give him a piece of my mind when I could see that he was in conversation with Ellie, and she didn't look too happy about it."

"In what way?"

"She looked as if she didn't know what to do or say, and the professor was saying something about having come across an old newspaper report in some papers he was studying, and it concerned a very unfortunate case about someone called Dawson. A bad fault, he said. He said there were deaths involved."

"Did he mention any other names? Or say why this had anything to do with Ellie?"

"Not that I heard. He just made some remark about a peculiar coincidence of names, and said that if there were any hint of incompetence in the

115

future, he was certain that sparks would fly."

"Did you hear Ellie say anything in reply to this?"

"Unfortunately, no," said Annette with regret. "Because somebody next to me chose that very moment to spill a drink, not over me, thank goodness, or I'd have had something to say to them in no uncertain terms, but with all the kerfuffle, the next time I looked, Ellie was sitting by herself on the other side of the room and the professor was talking to someone else. But it looked to me as if whatever the professor had said had given Ellie something to think about. Perhaps she'd had a shock. Oh!" Another little giggle. "I've made another little joke, haven't I?"

"Oh yes. Very good." Tania managed to rustle up a semblance of a smile. "It begins to sound to me as if Professor Kates went around making some very odd and oblique remarks to people during what was supposed to be a light-hearted social event."

"He did really," said Annette reflectively. "But not only to the young girls. Perhaps that was just his way with his students. Not that there's any excuse for a man like that to use his position to bully people. And he couldn't do that with somebody like that nice Roland."

"Roland Tighe, the butcher, you mean? You're saying that Professor Kates had some sort of conversation with him?"

"If you can call it a conversation," replied Annette. "I didn't think it sounded what you'd call friendly at all."

"I know Roland. I'm a regular customer at his shop. And my husband swears by his sausages."

"Hmmm. Not the only swearing that was going on on Saturday night, or else my ears deceive me," muttered Annette.

116

"From what I know of Roland, he's very much the type who can stand up for himself," observed Tania, intrigued. "So what was it all about? That's if you chanced to overhear anything by accident, of course," she added swiftly.

Annette had given up all pretence that her eavesdropping had been accidental. "Oh, Tania, my dear, you'll never get anywhere in this world if you don't keep your eyes and ears open. Which of course I was doing on Saturday night. Nothing to do with what happened later, you understand," she said hastily. "No, I mean about the murder mystery game that we were all going to be playing. If there's one thing I enjoy, it's a good whodunnit. I think I must be one of your best customers for those. Agatha Christie and Ngaio Marsh and Dorothy Sayers and all the rest of them. One of my favourite things is to try to pick up the clues as I'm reading so that I can work out the solution before the detective in the book does. And that was my plan on Saturday, you see."

Tania gave Annette a somewhat puzzled look. "Sorry, I don't quite see what this has to do with Roland Tighe."

"I'm just coming to that. You see, I was keeping my ears pricked in case anyone had picked up a clue that I'd missed. And I heard the word 'killer' quite clearly, so I looked around to see who'd said it, and it was Roland. Now you're right, of course – he is a very nice man, and he does have some beautiful meat in his shop, although I can't always afford it, because the supermarket does have some very good special offers, doesn't it? Anyway, it turns out that when he said 'killer', he was talking about an idea for a book that he's thinking about writing. A Victorian mass-murderer, or so I believe,

117

which seems unlikely for a man who is always so polite to his customers. Not that he sounded so polite the other evening."

"But in what way?" persisted Tania, who was exerting her best efforts not to sound impatient at Annette's ramblings. "When was this?"

Annette considered. "I'm almost sure that it was during our first break. Yes, it must have been, because otherwise there wouldn't have been any clues revealed for me to pick up. It sounded as if Roland was speaking to somebody – I'm not sure who – about his idea for a book, and Professor Kates was standing at his shoulder, and he butted in and said that the court files were full of details of people who had killed, and sometimes people who had come within a whisker of doing so. Roland said that he was only interested in one specific instance, and the professor said that, funnily enough, he'd come across a particular war-time record lately. A butcher just like Roland, as it happened. A very close-run thing, he called it. And he said that any butcher who was convicted of inappropriate practices would certainly be dead meat, and he gave a little sneering chuckle at his own joke, such as it was. Wouldn't that make a good story, he said. And Roland said that he should mind his own bloody business – excuse my French, Tania – and the professor said, didn't that describe Roland's own work perfectly, and that a bloody business was what he was hoping to avoid. And then he turned on his heel and stalked off, leaving Roland looking rather red-faced."

Before Tania could comment, the phone on her desk rang. "Hello, Ramston Library," she answered, sounding slightly relieved at the distraction. "... I'm sorry. I can't offhand remember if we have that in

118

stock. Just let me put you on hold for a moment while I check the catalogue." She pressed a button on the phone and looked back at Annette. "Sorry, Annette, but I'm going to have to deal with this customer."

"But Tania, what about Caroline? There were other things ..." protested the elderly lady.

"It's been lovely chatting to you," interrupted Tania firmly, "and I'll certainly let you know when I've tracked down that book you came in for."

"Did I?" Annette sounded puzzled.

"The one about Richard III?"

"Oh yes, that." An embarrassed smile. "I'd quite forgotten ..."

"So you really must excuse me." Tania turned to her computer monitor with determination, and after a few seconds hesitation, Annette turned disconsolately away and made her way out of the library. After a few clicks, Tania returned to the phone. "No, I'm afraid we don't have that here, but it is in stock at one of the other county branches, so if you like, I can order it in for you ... that's no trouble at all. So, do you have your library card to hand ...?"

Chapter 11

"I don't suppose there's a young lady here who fancies accepting an invitation to lunch?" murmured Ron huskily, causing Tania to jump slightly as she looked up from her desk.

"As it happens, you would be quite wrong, sir," smiled Tania coquettishly. "In fact, nothing would give me greater pleasure."

"Bad morning?" enquired Ron, detecting a tone of weariness in his wife's voice.

"I've spent the last hour trying to track down a missing consignment of books that were supposed to have been despatched from county central stores last week, except that nobody's seen hide nor hair of them."

"Sounds like another case for your brilliant detective skills," quipped Ron with a grin.

"Don't!" Tania gave a mock shudder. "I should have known it was going to be a trying morning when Annette Curtin turned up first thing. She practically battered the doors down in order to bring me her latest gossip. And if I hadn't had other things to deal with, I dare say she'd be here still."

"Ah, but did she have juicy information to reveal?" asked Ron. "If I've gathered anything about Annette, she was bursting with information."

"Actually, she was," admitted Tania reluctantly. "Not that I've had a chance to process it yet. But it turns out that she managed to overhear quite a few snippets on Saturday night, and I'm sure that in amongst them, there could well be something significant. And from her parting words about Caroline Cash, I have a funny feeling that she could have more up her sleeve."

"She's not still here now, is she?" wondered Ron,

casting a look around the library. "Lurking behind the bookshelves in the hope of picking up something juicy?"

Tania laughed. "No, I managed to shoo her away. But she'll probably be back."

"Then I suggest we make our escape while we can. How does lunch over at the abbey café sound? It's likely to be quiet, so you can bring me up to date."

"Good idea," agreed Tania. "Susie!" she called to her assistant, Jenny's weekday equivalent, a mumsy forty-something-year-old with frizzy blonde hair who was straightening chairs halfway up the room. "The desk's yours. I'm off to lunch. See you later."

*

The Holy Grail café was the refreshment room of Ramston Abbey, handily situated a short walk across the Market Square from Tania's place of work. Tucked away between two of the nave's buttresses on the site of the old cloisters, demolished at the time of the Reformation, it provided the abbey's visitors, and those of the locals who were in the know, with a selection of hot drinks and light meals, including a legendary brie-and-cranberry panini which was one of Ron's favourite snacks. The establishment was run by a team of ladies, all volunteers, headed by Sharon Burley, a comfortable-looking forty-five-year-old supply teacher whose reputation for baking the best cakes for miles around was well-deserved.

Pushing open the door, Tania and Ron found that the café was as quiet as Ron had anticipated, being occupied only by a solitary anorak-wearing couple who were in the process of rising from their table, dotted as it was by empty coffee cups and what looked like the remains of a couple of Sharon's famous sticky buns. As the visitors made their way out of the door, Sharon emerged from the kitchen to bid them a smiling 'Thank you, my loves. Cheerio!', before turning her attention to the new arrivals.

"Well, Tania," she greeted them, hands on hips and a wry smile on her friendly features. "Sounds as if you've got yourself another murder."

Tania raised her eyebrows. "You've heard, then?"

Sharon gave her generous jolly laugh. "What do you think? You can't keep anything quiet in a place like Ramston. I hadn't been open two seconds before dear old Louise Froyle, armfuls of flowers as usual, came bustling in to tell me somebody had been killed. Not again, I thought. But not here again, thank goodness, or I'd probably be the one telling her. She said that she'd been in to collect her usual Monday morning flowers from Thanks A Bunch over on the corner of the Square, and she'd heard that there had been a murder at the Town Hall on Saturday night, and it was something to do with the library."

"Not exactly," replied Tania. "And it wasn't anything to do with me. It was in the old library reading room in the main Town Hall building. The Literary Society were having a social function, and my assistant Jenny Chandler was working as a waitress when one of the Society's members was suddenly discovered to have been killed, and I happened to be working late, so Jenny came rushing through in a state to fetch me. But the police came just afterwards, so everything is in their hands now."

"Oh really?" Sharon responded with a sceptical look. "Are you sure about that?"

"Absolutely," stated Tania firmly.

"Because if I know anything about Tania Faye," continued Sharon as if Tania had not spoken, "she's not going to let a murder that's occurred under her nose be left to the police without at least taking an interest. I mean, look at that business in Cornwall, and then what happened in this very building. Didn't the police tell you to keep clear and leave things to them?"

"It's true. They did, didn't they, love?" said Ron. "Actually, they've done the same this time."

"And yet, by all accounts," swept on Sharon, "didn't they end up grateful that you'd used your brain to help sort out who was responsible?"

"They did," admitted Tania.

"So don't try and tell me that you're just going to stand by and not take a healthy interest, because I shan't believe a word of it. Especially," smiled Sharon, "as, from what I hear, the murder victim is a professor from Camford University. Another one! Seems to me you're making something of a speciality in them."

"It's hardly Tania's fault if Camford professors keep getting themselves killed in Ramston," laughed Ron.

"No," agreed Sharon, "but it might be her fault if whoever did this never gets caught." She took a look at Tania. "In fact, I wouldn't mind betting that you've already started trying to work out who it might have been."

Tania couldn't stop herself blushing. "Well, I might have had a talk with a couple of people who were there ..."

"I knew it!" declared Sharon. "And you've come in here, away from everybody, to chew over what you've found out."

123

"Actually," said Ron, "we've come in here to chew over some lunch, if that's okay by you."

"Honestly, what am I like?" Sharon cast her eyes to heaven. "Here's me keeping you talking, and all you want is something to eat. Sorry, dears. So, what can I get you?" She took a look at Ron. "As if I couldn't guess."

"You are a very astute woman," smiled Ron. He turned to his wife. "And for Madame?"

"I'll have the same please, Sharon. And a couple of fizzy waters too."

"Keeping your head clear for the investigation, eh?" chuckled Sharon. "Right. Two brie-and-cranberry paninis with side salad coming up. You two just sit down, and I'll bring them over." She disappeared into the kitchen as Ron and Tania took a table discreetly tucked away in a corner.

"So." Ron leaned forward eagerly. "What pearls did Annette Curtin let drop?"

"I shall ignore the implied reference to casting pearls before swine," responded Tania with mock huffiness.

"Sorry, love," said Ron contritely. "Bad choice of words. How would 'pearls of wisdom' suit you?"

"I may allow you to get away with it this time," said Tania graciously. "Actually, I'm not sure that wisdom is Annette's principal stock-in-trade. And there was a great deal of twittering. But she had picked up a few morsels of information when she was going about with her ears out on stalks."

"Such as?"

"For a start, Professor Kates seems to have had some sort of downer on the younger women in the Literary Society."

"Didn't approve of their writing styles? Not academic enough?"

"No, nothing like that. It seemed to have something to do with their jobs. He sounds to have had some sort of obsession with ploughing through old records, from what Annette heard, and he was making pointed remarks about Ellie Dee's work and Donna McIntosh's employment prospects. I have no idea why he would be interested in such things."

"Or why there would be any sort of motive for either of them to want to knock him over the head. Not that it would have been out of the question for either of them," reflected Ron. "A policeman's truncheon is a pretty solid thing, and Donna McIntosh looks a pretty little wisp of a girl, but you never know what reserves of strength someone is going to rustle up in a moment of crisis. And Ellie Dee seems quite a solid character. You can't go clambering up ladders and sorting out electrics if you haven't got a bit of power to your elbow."

"Speaking of which," said Tania, "Annette also heard the professor in some sort of confrontation with Roland Tighe."

"Would that be the same one that Jenny mentioned?"

"I wouldn't know about that. But Roland's certainly someone who could swing a mean cleaver if he put his mind to it."

"Shame the professor wasn't struck down with one of Roland's choppers," quipped Ron. "You'd have the case solved in two seconds."

"Not really funny, Ron," said Tania. "I like Roland. I don't like to think of him as a possible murderer."

"Well, it was one of them," pointed out Ron reasonably. "So what was it that was said between him and the professor that puts him in the frame?"

"According to Annette, there was something

about dead meat and a bloody business. Which of course is what Roland's all about, so whether Professor Kates was looking down on him because he's in a job where he gets his hands dirty, I can't see."

"And again, who kills someone because they make disparaging remarks about their work? Which sounds as if it could apply to any of the three."

Tania shrugged. "Who knows? But that's all I've got so far."

"Here you are, my dears," announced Sharon as she arrived with their plates of food. "And I'll be back in two seconds with your drinks. Oh, and one thing, Ron." She leaned in conspiratorially. "I may have had a run on sticky buns this morning, but I've got just one left. I don't suppose you'd like me to put your name on it?"

"You are a wicked temptress, Sharon," laughed Ron. "But I may just have a corner left after I've finished this."

"Let me know," twinkled Sharon, and disappeared back into the kitchen.

*

"That," said Ron, as he dabbed his mouth with his napkin and downed the last of his drink, "was delicious. I haven't had a panini like that since ... well, since the last one." He checked his watch. "And still plenty of time to polish off my sticky bun and then go for a constitutional round the Square before you have to be back in harness." He glanced up at the sound of the entrance door opening and dropped his voice to a murmur. "Actually, we may have to put that on hold. Don't look now, but you'll never guess who's just come in."

Tania, her back to the door, gave her husband a

126

quizzical look. "Astonish me."

"Caroline Cash. Didn't you say Annette wanted to say something about her?"

"Yes, but I never gave her the chance," replied Tania in similarly lowered tones. "Oh well, never mind. I shall have to busk it. Strike while the suspect is hot, and all that." She swung round in her chair and put on a bright smile. "Caroline!" she called. "Nice to see you."

Carrie, about to speak to Sharon who had emerged from her kitchen at the sound of the door, looked round in surprise. "Oh, Tania. Hello. I didn't notice you there."

"We came in for a bite of lunch. Please, join us."

"But I only popped in for a quick sandwich. I've just shut the shop for a few minutes. And I wouldn't want to impose ..."

"Nonsense," declared Ron. "Come and sit down. We can have a little chat." He pulled up a chair which Carrie, after giving Sharon her order, occupied with an apparent degree of reluctance.

"So, how have you been?" enquired Tania solicitously, as Sharon deposited a plate in front of the other woman. "Saturday must have been awful for you. The killing, that is."

"What do you mean?" responded Caroline, sounding startled. "Why do you say 'for me'?"

"I mean, for anyone," said Tania. "After all, it isn't every day that there's a murder you get caught up in. Anyone, I mean – not you in particular, of course."

"Oh. No. That's true, I suppose." Caroline's voice was still shaky.

"I wouldn't exactly say I'm lucky, but I have been involved with a couple of murder cases," continued Tania. "One of them when Ron and I actually discovered the body. Awful. Seeing someone dead. But I don't expect anything like that has ever happened to you before."

"No," replied Carrie. "It hasn't."

"So it's all bound to come as a shock. It would to anyone. That's why I was rather surprised to see you here. I wouldn't have blamed you if you'd decided to give work a miss today."

"I wanted to carry on normally as if Saturday night had never happened," said Carrie. "I wish I could forget all about it."

Tania shook her head. "So hard to do. Especially if you were friends with the person who's been killed. Tell me, were you and Professor Kates particularly close?"

"No," replied Carrie hastily. "No, not at all. In fact, I hardly knew him. I really hadn't had much to do with him at all."

"Oh, how odd." Tania furrowed her brow. "Because I'm sure someone told me that you and the professor had had quite the conversation earlier in the evening."

"Did we? I really don't remember ..."

"Wasn't it about one of the clue items in the murder game? Something about a diamond necklace? Or jewellery in general. Wasn't it said to have been stolen? Because of course, if there was going to be any talk of jewellery, you'd naturally be the one to speak to. Wasn't the professor talking about looking further into that? Or am I thinking of something else?"

"No, love," intervened Ron. "That was something Alex told us. It was just a murder clue. Nothing to do with Caroline at all."

"Oh. Good." Carrie sounded unaccountably relieved.

"So would that have been the only encounter you had with the professor during the course of the evening?" asked Tania. "You didn't see him, for instance, during the time that the party broke up to go up to the mayor's parlour for the main course of supper?"

Carrie shook her head. "No, I didn't see him at all."

"She wouldn't have, love," pointed out Ron. "Don't you remember, according to what we've heard, the professor went back downstairs pretty much straight away because he didn't fancy the quiche on offer?"

"Of course. I'd forgotten that," smiled Tania. "How silly of me!" Only one who knew them well would detect that Tania and Ron were employing their acting skills, so long honed during their membership of the Ramston Operatic And Dramatic Society, to construct a little scenario. "So where were you then, Carrie?"

"Now we know that too, love," remarked Ron indulgently. "She forgets everything, you know," he smiled to Carrie. "Didn't Ivan tell us ...?

"Of course! You're right. He did. Carrie ...?

"Ivan. Yes. That's right. Ivan wanted a cigarette, and we went outside."

"Told you!" said Ron in triumph. "So what exactly happened then, Carrie?"

Carrie looked perplexed. "I don't know what you're getting at. We had a smoke, and then we went back inside."

"Together?" enquired Tania guilelessly.

"Actually, no. I finished my cigarette first, and so I went back in."

"To do what?"

"I don't know." Carrie was beginning to sound

129

flustered. "Go to the loo? Get a drink? How can I be expected to remember every second of the evening? A man died. It doesn't help the memory, you know."

"No, of course not," soothed Tania. "But I expect you'd remember if you saw Professor Kates again at that time. So did you?"

"I don't think so. No, no I didn't."

"You didn't go back into the reading room for any reason?"

"I've told you, no."

"And you left Ivan outside. Did you see him come back into the Town Hall foyer?"

Carrie put her hand to her brow. "I can't remember. I wasn't paying attention. And why are you cross-examining me anyway? Why aren't you talking to some of the others, like Roland Tighe. He had just as much to do with the professor as I did." She took a breath. "Look, do you mind if I go? I really can't leave the shop any longer." Without another word, she pushed back her chair and made a hurried exit, leaving her sandwich untouched on the table.

Ron looked up at the clock above the counter. "And you'd better get back to work as well, love, or you'll be getting hard looks from Susie. You'd better hope she hasn't been inundated with customers in your absence. Or, even worse, the return of Annette Curtin."

"Oh, she'd cope," laughed Tania, getting to her feet. "And as for Annette, I'm sure she'll be back for an encore before long."

"So, shall I pick you up from work at the usual time? You do still close at five-thirty on a Monday, don't you?"

"We do, but why don't you make it ten minutes

early today? There's never usually anybody left in the library last thing, and I have an idea."

"And what might that be?"

"Wait and see." With a mysterious smile, Tania headed for the Holy Grail's exit.

Chapter 12

At five-twenty on the dot, Ron arrived in the library to find Tania virtually forcing her colleague to leave early.

"Go on, Susie," Tania was saying. "There's not a soul about, and it'll make up for some of those occasions when we've had to stay on a few minutes extra because somebody was taking their time about choosing books. I won't tell the council Chief Executive if you won't. Now, off you go." An encouraging smile accompanied her words.

"Well, if you're absolutely sure," said Susie, and made for the door, with a still-reluctant glance behind her as she left.

"So, mysterious one, what are you up to?" enquired Ron. "You evidently have a cunning plan. Am I allowed to share it?"

"Of course," said Tania, picking up her handbag, switching off the last of the lights, and bustling Ron towards the exit, locking the library front door firmly behind her. She looked at the Town Hall clock above their heads. "Good. Just in time."

"In time for what?" queried Ron.

Tania took his arm and started walking. "In time to pop round the corner and just catch Roland Tighe before he closes his shop, so that we can pick up something for supper, which you had unaccountably forgotten to buy."

Ron laughed. "You, my darling, are a remarkably crafty woman. How on earth do you come up with these ideas?"

"We have to have some sort of explanation for going around and talking to these people," replied Tania reasonably. "And this one just popped into my head at lunchtime, after Carrie had mentioned

132

Roland."

"I think you're wasted as a librarian," remarked Ron. "Instead of cataloguing books, I reckon you ought to be writing them. With a talent for plotting like yours, you'd make a fearsome whodunnit author."

"Oh no!" protested Tania. "I'm happy to read them, but real-life murder is a bit of an off-putter when it comes to creating them. Now shush. Here's Roland's shop."

The couple arrived outside the establishment just as Roland Tighe's young colleague was winding up the red-and-white striped awning over the shop's frontage.

"Hello, Gabe," Ron hailed the youngster. "Not too late, are we?"

"You're just in time, sir," replied Gabe. "Mr Tighe's inside, but I don't think he's cashed up yet."

"Oh good," said Tania, and led the way into the shop, where Roland looked up in surprise.

"Hello, Tania. You're cutting it fine, aren't you? I was just about to close up."

"I hoped we'd catch you," smiled Tania. "It's just that Ron had forgotten to buy what he needed for supper tonight, so we scooted round."

"Oh yes? And what was it that you needed, Ron?" asked Roland.

"Er ... um ... kidneys!" blurted Ron, caught unawares. "Yes, that's it. Kidneys. Tania loves devilled kidneys, and I was planning on surprising her." He turned to his wife with a broad grin. "We like to surprise each other, don't we, love?"

"Our life is full of surprises, isn't it, darling?" responded Tania with an answering grin.

"Right. Half a pound of lamb's kidneys coming up, if that suits you." Roland busied himself weighing up the items. "Now, is there anything else?" he enquired with a smile.

"Actually, Roland, there is," said Tania. "Could we have a word about what happened on Saturday night? I think there may be some things you can tell us."

Roland's smile faded. "I suppose," he said, not sounding particularly enthusiastic. "Gabe," he said to his young colleague, who was stowing the awning pole just inside the doorway. "Why don't you get off? I'll finish up here."

"Oh, okay, Mr Tighe. I'll just get my jacket. See you tomorrow." Gabe disappeared into the back room, and there came the sound of the back door slamming.

"Just let me close up, and then we won't be disturbed," said Roland. He closed the shop front door, stowed the keys in the front pocket of his apron, and gestured his visitors through into the back room.

Tania came straight to the point. "You had some sort of confrontation with Professor Kates on Saturday night, didn't you?"

Roland seemed taken aback at the bluntness of the question. "I don't know what makes you think that," he replied. "We were all just there to enjoy a pleasant social evening. And I've already given a statement to the police. I've told them everything I know."

"Everything?" Tania sighed. "Roland. I'm not trying to trap you into anything. All I want to do is get to the bottom of what happened in what I can't help thinking of as my library. Now I know that, strictly speaking, it's nothing to do with me – Detective Inspector Bright made that clear in no uncertain terms – but murder is a horrible thing.

And some of the people involved are friends of mine. I can't just stand by and do nothing."

Roland gave a small wry smile. "With the reputation you've managed to acquire for yourself, Tania, I'd be surprised if you did. I expect there are quite a few people around Ramston who are thinking that you seem to be pretty talented in sorting out murder mysteries."

Tania echoed the smile. "So can we start again?"

Roland nodded. "Sorry. Of course. And yes, you're right. The professor and I did have words on Saturday night. And I wouldn't mind betting that, once the police get to hear of it, that will make me a suspect. It's bound to."

"Exactly," said Ron. "So if I were you, I'd be telling Tania everything there is to know. What's the saying? 'The truth will set you free'?"

"I'm not sure how that's going to work," said Roland. "But go on. Tell me what you want to know."

"You were overheard in a couple of exchanges with the professor," said Tania. "Now I know that not everyone overhears everything accurately, so maybe you can clarify things for me."

"Things like what?"

"For instance, someone heard an exchange between you and the professor when he mentioned a record he'd come across involving an old case. Not, I think, one of his own, because of course he was a magistrate. But it was something to do with a shopkeeper during the war, and he referred to the case having a bad smell, and wanting to put some meat on the bones. Do you have any idea what he might have been referring to?"

Roland's face showed no expression. He shook his

head. "Sorry. I really can't remember."

"Now that seems odd," said Tania. "Because from the references he was making, it sounds very much as if he was talking about someone in the same line of business as yourself. Of course, yours is a family firm that goes way back, isn't it? And it sounded as if you were rather unsettled by the conversation."

"I don't know what you mean by 'unsettled'," responded Roland. "I really didn't have the faintest idea what the old fool was on about."

"That sounds rather as if you didn't particularly like Professor Kates," suggested Ron.

"To be honest, I didn't," said Roland. "Not that I ever had much to do with him. It wasn't as if he came to every meeting of the Society, but when he did he always seemed ready to look down on the rest of us. I mean, one time it got mentioned that I was thinking about writing a book about a Victorian murderer, and he just looked round and said 'Nothing ever gets done if you just think about it, my dear chap. That's pathetic. If you want to get anything done, you must take action'. He could sneer for England, that one."

"It's the sort of put-down that might make a man harbour a grudge," mused Tania. "A person might be moved to take actual action. So did you?"

"What? Kill him? No!" replied Roland hotly. "Why would I do that?"

"Because," said Tania, "that wasn't the only occasion where Professor Kates chose to get on the wrong side of you. I'm told he did it for a second time the other evening."

"You have had your spies out, haven't you, Tania?" Roland was beginning to sound somewhat less friendly. "Who's been dropping me in it this time/"

"I'm not going to name any names. It's what happened that concerns me. And this occasion specifically involved mention of a butcher's shop. I understand that the phrase 'dead meat' was used."

"Oh, that!" Roland gave a bark of dismissive laughter. "Well, I know where that's come from. I remember Annette Curtin was hanging about with her ears flapping, desperately trying to hone in on some gossip, just like she usually does."

"Who told me is not the point, Roland," replied Tania severely. "But if there was some kind of threat uttered, then that could be significant."

"I didn't threaten the professor," protested Roland. "Nothing of the kind. That woman's making it up."

"Nobody said that you threatened Professor Kates. But it sounded rather more as if he was threatening you."

"Well, how could he do that?" scoffed Roland. "Give away my secret sausage recipe?"

Tania did not look amused. "I think it sounded more serious than that, Roland. As I understand it, he mentioned the word 'conviction'. Again, as a magistrate he would have had access to all sorts of legal records. Was he threatening you with a conviction over something? Or had he perhaps found something in the past? Why might he be talking about a bloody business? Did he know or suspect something that might mean that you or your business would be 'dead meat'?"

"This is all madness," blustered Roland. "The only 'bloody business' anyone talked about was me telling the old fool to mind his own. If he wanted to make trouble, he'd come to the wrong person. And if someone else wants to make trouble for me, they know what they can do." He took a deep intake of breath. "And now, if you will excuse me, I should like to finish closing up." He picked up the parcel of kidneys and thrust them into Ron's hand. "And don't forget your dead meat."

*

"Well, what do you make of all that?" enquired Ron as he and Tania made their way back to their car.

"I honestly don't know," replied Tania.

"It was a game of two halves, wasn't it?" remarked Ron. "He started off as the affable Roland that we've always been used to, but I've never seen him turn snappy the way he did."

"He's bound to be feeling the strain," pointed out Tania. "After all, from what he said, he realises that he has to be under suspicion – or at least, he will be once the police get to hear about the words that passed between him and the professor on Saturday night. And they're sure to do so, once the Ramston gossip machine gets into full swing."

"Is that a not-so-subtle reference to Annette?" smiled Tania.

"I can't think of anyone more likely to be spreading anything that comes to her ears. And let's face it, those ears seem to be kept pretty busy. Almost as busy as her mouth. And didn't she say that she had more to tell you before you managed to stop her in mid-flow?"

"She did. And I'm sure she'll find an opportunity to fill in the gaps soon enough," said Tania resignedly.

"But coming back to what she said about Roland, doesn't that fit in with what Jenny said about Roland and Kates's little spat? Which definitely made him very jumpy. I for one am not buying what he says about not having a clue as to what the

138

professor was on about. The question is, what was the point of Kates's remarks? They obviously meant something. So has our Roland got a guilty secret hiding in his past, or his family's past, and if so, what on earth could it be?"

"Was there anything significant in the professor's choice of words?" wondered Tania. "Apart from an evident talent for making bad puns about the butchery trade?"

"I don't suppose you've got the sort of access the professor had to the kind of records he seems to have been looking at?"

"There are limits to what even a head librarian can research, darling," replied Tania. "Looks as if we're stuck with deduction and interpretation."

"At which you excel," grinned Ron. "And I'm not sure I believe you. If anyone can put a jigsaw puzzle together, it's you."

"And don't forget, we haven't got all the pieces yet," pointed out Tania. "We still have quite a few people to talk to. Somehow. And without falling foul of Inspector Bright."

"Good thought. But in the meantime," said Ron, "I'm carrying a parcel of lamb's kidneys which seems to be growing soggier by the minute. So I suggest we get home as soon as possible so that I can get to work in the kitchen. Kidneys do not devil themselves, you know. And you can pour a glass of wine and think clever thoughts about your next move." He held the car door open for his wife.

"I'll do my best," smiled Tania. "So, home, James."

*

"Though I sez it as shouldn't," announced Ron, laying down his knife and fork, "those kidneys were devilishly good."

Tania closed her eyes and emitted a groan of

139

mock anguish. "And they said comedy was dead."

"No, love," grinned Ron. "It's just been seriously unwell." He stood. "I shall load these plates into the dishwasher, and then what would you say to a coffee and a brandy?"

"I'd say 'Hello ...'" twinkled Tania, but her husband forestalled her.

"Don't you dare! I do the jokes round here."

"Then I shall adjourn to the living room and sit quietly while you make the drinks," said Tania demurely.

Some minutes later, Ron placed the tray of drinks on the coffee table and settled himself on the sofa next to his wife. "So, love, what next?" he enquired. "Any more thoughts as to what we know so far?"

Tania shook her head. "No, and I'm not intending to do any analysing until we've had a chance to speak to the rest of the people who were at the Town Hall on Saturday night. We're not even half-way down the list of suspects yet."

"So who's left? The three other women, I suppose. And how do you propose to get hold of them? In a way that doesn't start raising Inspector Bright's hackles," warned Ron.

Tania pondered for a moment. "You remember you wanted to get another power point fitted in the garage."

"I did?" Ron was puzzled.

"Oh yes. I'm absolutely certain you did," smiled Tania. "It had just slipped your mind for a moment. Now the thing is, you can't possibly do it yourself. Electricity is a dangerous thing. What you need is a qualified electrician." She sipped her coffee.

Ron caught on. "Isn't it convenient that we happen to know of one?" he grinned. "Do you suppose we ought to give her a call and see if she's free to fit a small job into her busy schedule?"

"What a good idea!" chuckled Tania in return. "Hold on." She reached for her phone and gave a series of dabs at the screen. "And there's her website. 'No job too small – call any time', she says. And there's her phone number." She pressed the 'call' key and passed the phone to her husband. "Over to you."

Ron, slightly startled at the speed of events, took the phone. "Oh, hello. Is that ED Electrics? ... Oh good. Sorry to call at this hour, but I've got a small electrical job that needs doing at home, and I wondered when you'd be free ... It's just a new power socket in my garage ... No, there's a single one there already, but I wanted a double ... I'm in Ramston, actually." He gave the address. "Can you really? That would be perfect. Er ... the name's Faye ... Well, I'll see you then." He clicked off the phone. "There's a bit of luck. She said it sounds like a five-minute job, and she can fit it in first thing tomorrow before her first appointment. She'll be here at quarter to nine." He took a swig of brandy.

"Well done, darling." Tania leaned across and gave her husband a kiss. "I knew your brilliant acting talents would come to the fore."

"Okay, that's one tick on your list. Any more crafty ideas?"

"How about," suggested Tania, "if I call his chambers, once we've finished with Ellie Dee, and see if I can get an appointment to see Jack Hughes? Goodness knows whether he's going to be in court, or if he'll even see me at all, but I'm sure I can rustle up some pretext or other to get a word with him."

"Here's a thought. You're worried about your junior colleague Jenny because she's terrified that

141

she's in danger of being suspected of the murder, and you want to reassure her?"

"And you accuse me of being the devious one?" laughed Tania. "Although ..." She reflected briefly. "Actually, I might be able to pull that off. As a concerned employer, of course."

"And given your own brilliant acting talents, don't forget, love."

"Crawler!" Tania gave her husband a playful swat. "I'll call him in the morning. And then maybe we can get round to someone else later."

"Such as Monica de Glenn? What if you wanted her to paint a portrait of your dear old Auntie Ethel's pet pug to give her for her hundredth birthday? I'm sure I've seen adverts for her doing that sort of thing in the local rag. Is that worth a shot?"

"I'm beginning to think that brandy's gone to your head," replied Tania with a smile.

"On the contrary," retorted Ron. "I do some of my best thinking when I've got a tot or two of brandy under my belt. I recommend it. So you stay put, and I shall fetch the bottle." He heaved himself to his feet and headed for the kitchen.

Chapter 13

At quarter to nine on the dot, the doorbell rang.

"I'll get that," said Ron swiftly. "You'd better make yourself scarce. We should try not to be too obvious about this."

"Good idea," replied Tania, and disappeared upstairs as Ron answered the door, to find Ellen Dee standing on the doorstep, toolbox in hand and a friendly smile on her face.

"Mr. Faye? I'm Ellie. You called me yesterday."

"I did indeed. And you're perfectly on time. Such a change these days. I hate waiting in for people who say they'll turn up at a given time and then don't."

"Well, I'm here now. So how can I help? You said something about an electrical socket."

"You'd better come through." Ron led the way into the garage and gestured to the workbench. "There. It's just a single socket, and sometimes I need to plug two things in at once if I'm doing the garden, so I thought a double would be better."

"That's the easiest thing in the world," said Ellie. "Let me pop out to the van, and I'll be back in two seconds." She was true to her word, and within moments had returned, twin socket in hand. "And your fuse box is ..."

"Just up there." Ron pointed, and then stood back as Ellie began work. "Of course, I suppose I could have done it myself, but I'm always wary of electricity. So many things to go wrong, aren't there? And I know that, these days, you're meant to get everything done by a qualified electrician with all the paperwork."

"That's right," agreed Ellie absently as she concentrated on the job.

"Of course, I'm sure you've got all the necessary

143

certificates in place, so I don't need to worry."

There was a momentary hesitation. "Yes, that's right." A slightly awkward silence followed, before Ellie put down her screwdriver and stood back. "There you are, Mr. Faye. One double socket as requested."

"Marvellous. Exactly what I wanted," smiled Ron.

"Just let me do the paperwork ..." Ellie dived into her toolbox and produced a clipboard, before rapidly filling in a form and handing it over. "There you are. All official."

"Thank you very much. Let's just pop inside so that I can get my wallet. And you were so quick, I bet you've got time for a quick cup of tea. When's your next appointment?"

Ellie checked her watch. "Half-past nine. If you're sure ..."

"Perfect. My wife is a very good tea-maker." Ron headed for the kitchen, Ellie at his heels, to find Tania filling the kettle.

When her eyes fell on Tania, Ellie came to a sudden stop. "Oh. It's you, isn't it? From the library."

"Oh, hello. Ellie, isn't it?" responded Tania innocently. "Isn't that an odd coincidence? I knew my husband had arranged an appointment with an electrician, but I had no idea it was you. How nice to see you again." She assumed a solemn expression. "Such a change from last Saturday night. So how are you?"

Ellie seemed to be still processing the situation. "Oh, alright, I suppose."

"Getting on with things, I expect," said Tania warmly. "Good. Anyway, do sit down. We can have a little chat while Ron makes the tea."

"Will do, love." Ron kept an admirably straight

144

face as he complied.

Tania seated herself opposite Ellie at the kitchen table. "Of course, I'm not really involved, but I do feel some sort of sense of responsibility as what happened on Saturday night took place in my library, in a way. Well, what used to be, anyway. So I can't help wondering about everything that went on that evening. I mean, it all started out as a light-hearted social event, didn't it?"

"Yes, I suppose so." Ellie still sounded unsettled.

"And you were all playing along in your various characters. I know what fun that can be, because Ron and I are members of the Ramston Dramatic Society. What was your character again?"

"I was meant to be a TV weather girl," said Ellie.

"Oh yes, I remember," said Tania. "My friend Alex told me all about the characters people were playing. Funny, isn't it, that the actual weather girl was given another part to play? But I suppose that it wouldn't be as much fun if you were playing somebody who was too much like you."

"No?" Ellie seemed puzzled. She ignored the mug of tea which Ron placed soundlessly in front of her.

"For instance," continued Tania, "I don't suppose there are many electricians who get mixed up with suspicious deaths." A guileless smile.

This time, Ellie's reaction was unmistakeable. She caught her breath, and the colour drained from her face. "I ... I don't know what you mean."

"She means, it must have come as a dreadful shock on Saturday night when you all discovered that Professor Kates had been murdered," intervened Ron. "That's it, isn't it, love?"

"Yes, of course," said Tania gently. "And I don't imagine that Ellie had any reason to suppose that anyone could have some sort of motive to do the

145

professor harm. Least of all herself."

"No. No, of course not," insisted Ellie shakily.

"Tell me, did you happen to see him during the period you'd all broken the second time for supper? Because that's the time when the murder happened, isn't it? We know he left the mayor's parlour to go downstairs? Did you?"

"No," replied Ellie hastily. "Well ... yes, actually. I needed the loo."

"So when would that be?"

"I don't know." The young electrician seemed flustered. "Maybe twenty past nine. I don't know. Honestly."

"And you saw him then?"

"No. No, I didn't. Not at all." Ellie was insistent.

"Actually, how well did you know Professor Kates?" wondered Tania. "Apart from through the Literary Society?"

"Not at all, really. We'd hardly spoken."

"You surprise me. I mean, both being members of the same Society, I'd have thought you'd have quite a lot in common. Didn't he like what you wrote?"

"No," Ellie hastened to explain. "He didn't. That is, I didn't. Write, I mean. You see, I joined the Literary Society because I thought it was some kind of book club, which it is in a sort of way. Every month the committee chooses a book for us to read, and then at the meetings we discuss it and say what we like about it and what we don't. That's the bit I enjoy most, specially when it's a romantic novel. They're my favourites. We've been reading one lately. But whenever it was that kind of book and Professor Kates was at the next meeting, because he didn't always go, he was always the first to say that they were complete rubbish, and not worth the paper they were printed on, and he couldn't understand why anybody with any intelligence could enjoy them. He only read serious stuff."

"So when it came to literary appreciation, you and the professor weren't exactly on the same page," remarked Ron with a grin, earning him a severe stare from his wife.

"But that wouldn't be any reason for Ellie to wish the professor harm, darling," said Tania. "That wouldn't make any sense. And I'm sure you wouldn't be one to hold a grudge over something like that, would you, Ellie?"

"No. No, I wouldn't."

"Actually, now you come to mention the professor's reading habits," said Tania, "it seems as if there was something he'd read that he mentioned to you which sounded slightly odd."

"I ... I don't know what that would be." The unease was back in Ellie's voice.

"It was something that someone overheard during one of the breaks in proceedings at the murder evening, but it wasn't anything to do with the murder game, as far as I can gather. The person I heard it from told me that apparently, the professor was speaking to you and he made a comment about some old newspaper reports he'd been reading, and there was a reference to a story about a case where some people died, evidently as a result of some electrical wiring going wrong."

Ellie shook her head. "I don't remember anything about that," she insisted.

"No? You surprise me. Wasn't there a mention of someone called Dawson, Ron?" Tania turned to her husband for confirmation, to be answered with a nod. "Didn't the professor say something about a coincidence of names?"

"I still don't know what you mean." Ellie sounded

unsettled once again.

"And he said," went on Tania, "according to my informant, that if there were ever any hint of incompetence in any electrical work which led to unfortunate consequences, sparks would fly. All of which, by all accounts, left you looking rather stricken."

"But she would be, love," broke in Ron. "Nobody accused of incompetence would find that easy to cope with. And I'm sure there wouldn't be any hint of that with Ellie here. I was watching her work, and she looked very efficient to me. And not only that, but I've got her official certificate covering our little job, so I think we can sleep safe in our beds tonight. Isn't that right, Ellie?"

Ellie's reaction was to regard Tania and Ron blankly in turn, before looking up at the kitchen wall clock above Tania's head and seeming to come to with a start. "Oh, lord. Is that really the time? Look, I have to go. I'm going to be late for my appointment. Thank you for the tea." Without another word she picked up her toolbox and blundered hastily into the hall and out of the front door, pausing only to stow her tools in the back of her van before driving swiftly away with a crash of gears.

*

"And what," enquired Ron, having closed the open front door and seated himself in the vacant chair at the kitchen table, "do we think about all that?"

"Quite a few questions, and remarkably few explanations," responded Tania. "A virtual complete denial of everything that we've been told passed between her and the professor."

"Which could mean that she has a shocking

148

memory, or that she's hiding something."

"Everyone's hiding something," said Tania. "Don't you remember, Jenny told us that when the so-called detective inspector in the murder game said that everyone had a guilty secret, there was something of a pregnant pause in the proceedings? So it sounds as if he hit rather closer to the mark than he intended. And Ellie wasn't the first of our suspects to get jumpy when taxed with what passed between them and Professor Kates. And I have a feeling she may not be the last."

"Yet again, we've got the professor making oblique remarks which seem to rattle people, but not quite coming to the point," observed Ron. "And what's the relevance of this odd mention of somebody called Dawson? Who on earth is that? I can't fathom what he was about. It puts me in mind of the old saying, 'Willing to wound but yet afraid to strike'. What did he hope to gain?"

"Didn't somebody suggest he was on a power trip?"

"If we're talking about Ellie, isn't that the sort of appalling pun you expect from me?" smiled Ron. "I'll pretend I didn't hear it. So, what's next?"

"What's next is the fact that Ellie isn't the only one who risks being late for their job," pointed out Tania. "In fact, if I don't get my skates on, I shall be faced with a queue of irritated customers at the door of the library demanding to know why I've opened late."

"Better do something about that," said Ron, reaching for the car keys. "I shall go and fire up the chariot." He made his way out towards the garage.

*

Tania's fears did not prove true, and she arrived at the library in plenty of time. As she was just

149

settling behind her desk and opening her computer, her weekday assistant Susie arrived with news.

"I've just seen some policemen going into the Town Hall," she announced, "and they had a couple of those people in white overalls with them. It must be something to do with the murder. Do you know what's happening?"

"I don't," replied Tania. "There was nothing going on when I got here just now. Perhaps there's been a development. Are you okay to man the desk for a few minutes while I pop through?"

"Of course."

Tania made her way to the communicating door which led through to the main Town Hall building. Opening it carefully, she passed through, only to come face to face with Detective Inspector Bright.

"Well, well. If it isn't Mrs Faye," said the inspector, accompanying her words with a smile which was far from friendly. "And what, I wonder, brings you away from your own territory and on to my crime scene today?"

"Oh, just a healthy interest in what's going on around the building," said Tania lightly. "I heard that some of your people were here in the old library, which of course would once have been my own territory, and I wondered if there was any news."

"If there is, Mrs Faye, I shall make sure you'll be one of the last to know," sneered Bright. "As I told you, I don't appreciate interference in a case I'm working on, and if I were to find out that you'd been attempting to meddle in the investigation, I should take a very dim view of it."

"I wouldn't dream of getting in your way, inspector," said Tania with her most disarming smile. "But you must realise that the whole town is concerned about what happened here, and I'm being forever asked what I know. Wouldn't it be awful if I wasn't able to give simple answers to the questions that people naturally have? They'll only go and make up their own gossip, and who knows, that might even get in the way of your work."

"Hmmm. You may have a point," conceded the inspector grudgingly.

"So there must be something you can tell me," coaxed Tania. "Obviously, without giving away any sensitive information." She looked past the inspector. "For instance, I notice that you have some of your colleagues in overalls through in the reading room. Don't they call them SOCO? Scene Of Crime Officers, isn't it? I'd have thought that area would have been thoroughly examined by now."

"And it has been," grunted Bright.

"But I'm guessing with very little success, judging by the fact that your team are back again?"

"I think of it as being thorough."

Tania looked around. "I'm glad all that stripey police tape had been removed. Except for the exhibition area. Any special reason?"

"Merely that SOCO didn't get round to it initially. Limits on overtime." Bright gave an impatient 'tut'. "They'll get to it."

"More thoroughness?" smiled Tania.

Bright gave a resigned sigh. "It won't have escaped your notice that the exhibit is a kitchen scenario. I've lost count of the number of times that kitchen implements have been used as weapons. Knives, rolling pins – I even had one case where the murderer used a meat tenderiser. So we check."

"At least it's good to have the art gallery looking

151

more normal again. And I see that you've cleared away the table of so-called 'evidence' from the murder evening," noted Tania. "Not that it would have been actual evidence in the case of Professor Kates's murder, of course. Unless you were able to confirm that the police truncheon, rather than a supposed meat tenderiser, was in fact the actual murder weapon." She shot a glance at the inspector.

Despite herself, Inspector Bright gave a reluctant smile. "Mrs Faye, you are too sharp for your own good. And you know I cannot possibly confirm information of that kind."

"No, of course not," said Tania with an answering glint in her eye. "Just as I'm sure you wouldn't be able to tell me that there were no fingerprints on the truncheon, other than the prints of the two gentlemen who were organising the murder mystery evening." She raised an interrogative eyebrow, to which Bright responded with a long level look. "And I wouldn't mind betting," continued Tania, "that you probably took the fingerprints of everyone who was present on Saturday night, just for elimination purposes. And it's so much easier now than in the old days, isn't it? Those clever little scanners you use, I mean. So much less mess and fuss than having everyone press their fingers on to an inky pad and then leave a smudgy print on a piece of paper. Isn't it wonderful what you can pick up about police procedures just by watching those cosy crime programmes on television?"

"Mrs Faye," said the inspector, with the ghost of a smile. "Can I beg you, if you would be so kind, never to contemplate taking up a life of crime? At least, not on my patch."

"Oh, I'd never dream of such a thing, inspector," responded Tania airily. "No, I prefer to stay on the side of the angels, like yourself. Without the responsibility, of course. I mean, you have all the hard drudgery of going round to all the suspects in the case and checking over everything they've told you in their statements, just in case you find any discrepancies. Whereas I, since they're largely my friends, can simply chat to them in an ordinary way. I'm sure you couldn't find anything to object to in that." An innocent smile.

"Mrs Faye." The warning note was back in Inspector Bright's voice. "If I find out that you have been going around ..."

"Heavens!" interrupted Tania, looking at her watch. "I had no idea we'd been chatting so long. I'd better get back to the library, or they'll start thinking I've been arrested. And I've been keeping you from your work. So sorry. I must fly." Without a backward glance, she escaped though the pass door into the library, careful not to let the inspector see the satisfied smile on her face.

"Well?" enquired Susie as Tania resumed her seat behind the library front desk. "What's the news?"

"Nothing much," replied Tania. "They seem to be going over the reading room again in case they've missed anything, but I don't know that they have any great hopes. The detective inspector in charge was there. She couldn't really tell me anything – that's to say, she said she couldn't, but I managed to winkle a few facts out of her, so at least when people come asking, I can give them a little information."

"So, are you going to do any more investigating?" asked Susie.

Tania laughed. "You're getting as bad as Jenny.

And as a matter of fact, I am. So if you wouldn't mind checking that all the returned books from yesterday afternoon go back on the shelves, I have to make a quick phone call." As Susie went about her task, Tania turned to her computer screen and was soon able to bring up a phone number for Jack Hughes' law firm.

"Putnam Hinder Cage and Lockett," came the efficient-sounding voice down the line.

"Oh, good morning. I was wondering if Mr Hughes happened to be in the office today?"

"Yes, Mr Hughes is in Chambers at present," was the slightly frosty correction.

"Then I wonder if I might speak to him."

"May I ask what it's in connection with?"

"Yes. A case of murder."

"Oh." The voice was clearly taken aback. *"May I say who's calling?"*

"My name is Mrs Faye. Tania Faye."

"One moment please." Click, and a brief burst of Vivaldi before another click. *"Mrs Faye?"* came the voice of Jack Hughes. *"You're ... you're the librarian who came on the scene after the murder on Saturday night, I think. But I don't see that we have anything to discuss. I've given a statement to the police, and I have nothing further to say beyond that."*

"Well, that's the thing, Mr Hughes. You see, I've received some information regarding you from someone who was present that night, and I wonder if it might be wise to talk it over with you before mentioning it to the police."

There was a long pause. *"I see. Well, I suppose there's no harm in having a little chat."*

"Today? Lunchtime?"

"Um ... yes. But not here."

"What about the Cross Keys? One o'clock?"

"*Very well.*" Click.

'No 'goodbye' then?' thought Tania. 'Fine. Maybe I should get Ron in on this.' She picked up the receiver and dialled once more.

Chapter 14

"You said what?" Ron could scarcely contain his mirth. "And she bought it?"

Tania permitted herself a quiet smile. "You did commend me, darling, on my acting skills. So I was merely playing the part of a concerned librarian who was innocently asking questions about a baffling mystery which I'd somehow been accidentally caught up in. But to be frank, I don't think Inspector Bright bought it for a second. You don't get to be a senior detective on murder cases if you're that gullible. Actually, I have a sneaky suspicion that she was enjoying the verbal sparring. She even cracked a smile at one point. But for all that, I don't think she'd be too happy if she caught me getting deeply involved. Innocent questions are one thing. Muddying the waters would be quite another."

"Then you'd better not do any muddying," suggested Ron. "Stick to the innocent conversations."

"Yes, dear," said Tania with mock meekness.

"If we come across something that's impossible to explain away, though, she'll have to be told."

"Sufficient unto the day," replied Tania. "There's still loads we don't know."

"Anyway, what time's this chap supposed to be showing up?" asked Ron.

"One o'clock. And I'm due back at the library at quarter to two, so let's hope he's punctual."

Ron looked at his watch. "Those sandwiches ought to be here soon. We can eat while you detect."

The couple were seated in a quiet corner of the main bar of the Cross Keys Hotel, Ramston's

156

principal hostelry situated on the Market Square directly opposite the imposing bulk of the town's Norman abbey. As Tania had anticipated, being a Tuesday lunchtime, the bar was not particularly busy, and the pair had chosen a secluded booth tucked away at one extremity of the room, where sturdy stone walls and a profusion of massive oak beams ensured a considerable degree of privacy. As Ron had predicted, within moments the burly figure of Dennis Dean, the pub's landlord, arrived bearing two large plates.

"Two rounds of prawn specials as ordered," he announced in his robust local burr, laying down the plates with their contents of generously-filled sandwiches, a pile of crisps, and a small bowl of dressed salad.

"Thank you, Dennis. Goodness, this is a feast," remarked Tania.

Dennis laughed. "Well, you got to keep your strength up when you're detecting a murder, haven't you?" He lowered his voice. "I take it you're still on the trail of Ramston's latest killer, Tania. Getting anywhere, are you?"

"Early days, Dennis," smiled Tania in response. "Let's just say that some bits and pieces of information are coming my way. But whatever you do, don't let the police know. They don't take too kindly to us amateurs sticking our fingers into their pie."

Dennis tapped the side of his substantial nose with a finger. "Not a word from me, Tania. But if you don't tell me the whole story in due course, you're going to be in my bad books."

"It's a promise, Dennis," smiled Tania. "Now, as it happens, I'm expecting someone in here to have a little chat with on the subject any minute, so if

157

anyone comes looking for me, could you point them in our direction?"

"Course I will," replied Dennis. "Unless it's the police, that is." He went on his way chuckling.

Only a minute or so later, the figure of Jack Hughes appeared round the corner. "Mrs Faye, I think," he said. "And Mr Faye too, if I'm not much mistaken. I recognise you from the other night at the Town Hall. But to be honest, I'm not at all sure what I'm doing here."

"To be frank, Mr Hughes, *I* wasn't at all sure that you'd come. Perhaps you were intrigued by what I'd said earlier, about having some information which might be interesting to the police."

"Perhaps," responded Jack guardedly, and gave Tania a quizzical look. "So ...?"

"I imagine you must have known Professor Kates outside the Literary Society," began Tania, seemingly at a tangent. "With the legal connection, that is. You must have encountered him in court at some point, I would think."

"I have appeared in the magistrates court on occasion when he was on the bench," said Jack. "Not frequently. And certainly only at a professional distance." His tone continued to be wary.

"And what did you think of him?"

"As what?"

"As a person. Either in the courtroom context or at the meetings of the Literary Society. Did you like him?"

Jack looked faintly surprised at the question. He drew a breath. "Not that it seems particularly relevant, but since you ask, no. He was not an especially likeable man, in my opinion. He seemed to have a talent for putting people down." A grim

158

smile. "Or in some cases, sending them down. In the old days, if he'd reached the heights of the judiciary, he would probably been known as a 'hanging judge'. But as I say, I didn't really know him."

"He seems to have known you," said Tania lightly. "In some respects, anyway."

"How do you mean?" The guarded tone was back in Jack's voice.

"You say he was inclined to put people down," said Tania, declining to answer. "I wonder if he did the same to you regarding your writing. I assume you are involved in some sort of written output, as a member of the Society?"

The question seemed to unsettle Jack. "Actually, no. I mean, that's to say, I've had one or two thoughts about writing a book, but I've never actually presented anything to the other members, so Kates couldn't have commented. I mainly joined for the reading aspect of membership. And perhaps to pick up some tips on writing style. If I ever do write anything, that is."

"Ah. Well, we shall wait with interest to see, when you do eventually publish," smiled Tania. "So the remark I heard about must have been something to do with your professional work."

Jack shrugged. "Sorry. Doesn't ring a bell."

"Oh, most definitely. You see, the person who mentioned it to me seems to have been quite close to you at the time, and they have to make a point of being highly accurate in their work, so I don't think they would have been mistaken."

"Mistaken about what?" enquired Jack edgily.

"It was odd," said Tania. "Because it started out with some comment about fiction. Pure fiction in statements, I think the remark was, so it sounds

159

very much as if it was something to do with some event or other in court. Perhaps some defendant's statement had been shown to be full of holes, and both you and the professor happened to be involved in that case. I'm just guessing, of course. But then there was a reference to impure fiction – maybe the professor was making some sort of joke about this supposed statement. Was the professor in the habit of making jokes in court, do you know?" A guileless smile.

"Not to my knowledge," responded Jack flatly.

"Oh. Well, from what I've heard of him, probably not," said Tania. "But anyway, he apparently went on to talk about career advancement, and he said something about there being influential people who could be persuaded to help people in their careers under the right circumstances. I think he called them customers for a particular type of fiction. I suppose that might have been a reference to corrupt lawyers or something of the sort. Have you ever come across that kind of thing?"

"Certainly not," replied Jack sharply. "There's no room in the legal profession for anything like that. And I find it quite offensive that you should ask me the question."

"I'm sure Tania didn't mean to offend you, Mr Hughes," intervened Ron. "Or imply that your professional standards were anything but impeccable. She's just trying to work out an explanation for the professor's remark. And of course, as you say, you haven't written anything of a literary nature, so it couldn't have been anything to do with that. Odd, isn't it?"

"As you say. But as I've already told you, the conversation you've had reported to you doesn't ring a bell. I wonder if your source is entirely to be relied upon. Who was it, by the way?"

Tania smiled. "Oh, we librarians never reveal our sources," she replied lightly. "So really, there was only one other thing that I hoped you might be able to help me with."

"Really? Not that I can see why you want my help in any case. As you know, I've given my statement to the police. If there's anything you need to know, surely you can obtain the information from them." Jack adopted a faintly scoffing tone. "Although I have my doubts as to whether they would be particularly forthcoming to an ordinary civilian. Just a librarian, as you say, even if you are regarded, if I understand correctly, as something of a star amateur sleuth in the Ramston area."

Tania chose to take the observation as some sort of compliment, even though it was plainly not intended as such. "It's very kind of you to say so." She manufactured a bashful smile, which caused Ron to look away and bite his lip. "But it's the librarian in me that causes me concern. You see, my junior colleague Jenny – you'll remember, she was the waitress for the evening - is so upset, having been caught up in the events of Saturday, that I'm concerned to set her mind at rest. She is constantly worrying over who might have been responsible for the killing, since it can only have been one of the people who were in the room with her. So what I was hoping you could tell me was, did you leave the supper room during the period when the professor must have been murdered, or did you see anyone else do so? Just to ease Jenny's mind, of course."

Jack reflected. "I did, certainly. I went downstairs to take a look at the things on the so-called evidence table."

"Ah, now that's interesting," said Ron. "I suppose you were viewing them with a professional eye."

Jack gave a faint dismissive snort. "I think I probably left my professional eye at the door. As far as I was concerned, the evening was just a slightly comic attempt at a piece of crime fiction, so I looked at it in that light. But if I could win the promised champagne, I wasn't going to turn my nose up at it, so I thought I might as well play the game as best I could."

"So do you remember when you went down to look at the evidence items?" resumed Tania.

"Somewhere around quarter or twenty past nine, I suppose," said Jack. "It was just after that student boy and the antiques woman went down. They were going outside for a smoke, apparently."

"So you went to look at the evidence table. Did you notice anything in particular about it? Anything missing, for instance?"

Jack frowned. "No, not that I could see. I just glanced over the things, but there wasn't anything that I hadn't already picked up from when the detective chap had told us about them. And anyway, after a couple of minutes, Roland Tighe turned up, seemingly to do the same thing, so I just left him to it. I couldn't be bothered to go back up for any more food, so I just mooched about looking at some of the pictures around the gallery."

"And did you happen to see anyone else downstairs during that time?"

"Yes, actually. Not long after I came down I saw Ellie Dee come down the stairs, but she just disappeared straight into the loo. And I think it was Monica de Glenn who followed her down a minute or so later, but I've no idea where she went. Maybe to look at the evidence with Roland. I wasn't really paying attention."

"So you stayed downstairs in the gallery the whole time after that?" Tania sought to clarify.

"I was going to, but then I thought I'd get another drink before we started again, so I went back up to the mayor's parlour just shortly before the detective called us together to go back down again. After which … well, I assume you know what happened then."

"So that was it? You saw or heard nothing more?"

Jack frowned. "Odd you should ask. Not that I saw anyone or anything, but I did hear the professor say something. He had the sort of voice that carries."

"Yes, we've been told that," nodded Tania. "So who was he speaking to, and what was it that he said?"

"As to who, I have no idea. I couldn't see. But what he said was 'Almost perfect, but almost isn't good enough'. And I heard a door close."

"And you don't know what he meant?"

A shrug. "No clue. At the time I was more concerned with going to get another drink." Jack checked his watch. "Now, if you will excuse me, I have work to do." He gave a brittle smile as he stood. "You should be grateful that I didn't charge you for my time at my usual rate. These minutes could have cost you a great deal." Without another word, he was gone.

"And speaking of minutes," observed Ron, also consulting his watch, "you have five minutes to finish that sandwich before you turn into a librarian pumpkin at quarter to. So, what did you make of our lawyer friend?"

"I'm busy," replied Tania, concentrating on chewing. "You talk, I'll listen."

"Okay. So, first of all, we've got a few more details to add to your precious timeline. We've got confirmation of Ivan and Carrie's movements, at least when they went downstairs and out to have their smoke. We still haven't got anything about what they did afterwards. And we've also got confirmation that Ellie went down to go to the loo a few minutes afterwards. Again, we have no idea whether she was in there forever or just a short while. Knowing the way some women take a lifetime to go to the loo, she could even be in there still."

"Oi!" objected Tania through a mouthful of sandwich.

"Moving right along," continued Ron hastily, "we have new information. If what Jack Hughes has told us is correct, Monica went downstairs to the gallery just after Ellie, and Roland followed her a couple of minutes after that, which puts them both in the right area at the right time. Jack says he went back up to the parlour, but we haven't got anything on either of the others. So there we have quite a few people with the opportunity to be in the right place at the right time."

"And the list isn't even complete yet," pointed out Tania, finishing the final morsel and picking up her handbag. "People still to talk to, if we can figure out how to do it."

"And on the subject of talking," said Ron, as the couple made their way out of the door to a jolly 'Cheerio, you two. Can't wait to hear the latest' from Dennis Dean, "what about that remark by the professor that Jack overheard just before he headed upstairs? What do we think that means?"

"Unless we know who he was speaking to," said Tania, as the couple hurried across the Market

Square in the direction of the library, "we're somewhat in the dark. Just another piece of the jigsaw which will eventually fall into place. See you later." She deposited a peck on her husband's cheek and made her way into the building.

Chapter 15

It was just after five o'clock, and Tania was enjoying a few minutes of blessed quietness alone, taking the chance to re-shelve some returns, when the silence of the library was broken as Jenny Chandler surged through the front door.

"Tania, you'll never guess the latest," announced the dental nurse breathlessly.

"I don't suppose I will." Tania gave a good-humoured sigh. "At the moment, my guessing faculties are not at their sharpest."

It had been one of those afternoons. Almost as soon as Tania had returned to her desk after lunch, the phone had rung with a demand from County Library Headquarters in Westchester. Apparently the recent stock-check throughout the county's entire branch network – an activity which Tania had mercifully managed to complete at her own branch just before the revelations of the previous Saturday night – had thrown up a series of discrepancies, and those in command were demanding a complete audit of the entire system. Fortunately, Tania's meticulous record-keeping had allowed her to demonstrate a total command of the situation at her own library, and the work had proved relatively easy, if mind-numbingly dull, although it had still taken a substantial amount of time. There had followed a series of awkward customers with requests to trace the most obscure publications, which had necessitated a painstaking trawl through county, national, and even in one case international records and catalogues, before the customers could finally be sent on their way with differing degrees of satisfaction. And finally, to top it all, the mother-and-toddler reading group which met in the library every Tuesday afternoon had descended into chaos as no less than three of the children had simultaneously erupted in an orgy of projectile vomiting which had left the reading corner in an appalling state. As the mothers hustled their children, in varying states of cleanliness, out of the library, with profuse expressions of regret but a total absence of offers to help, Tania and her assistant Susie were left to attempt to restore order and clean up the aftermath of the incident. Finally, with the time approaching five o'clock, with the library's appearance and atmosphere restored to something like normal, and with an absence of visitors, Tania had told Susie to finish early, and her colleague had gratefully departed, leaving Tania alone.

Jenny's arrival shattered the calm, and she seemed oblivious to Tania's weary demeanour, bursting as she was to deliver her news. "We had one of our patients turn up in the surgery without an appointment today. Something about a loose filling, she claimed, but I'm sure it was just one of her usual ploys to spread some gossip and see if there was anything fresh to pick up."

Tania gave a laugh. "Oh, now I think I can guess which patient you're talking about. Annette Curtin."

"You see!" exclaimed a delighted Jenny. "I always said you were a brilliant detective."

"So which beans did Annette spill on this occasion?" asked Tania. "Funnily enough, when she was in here yesterday she was telling me, in great detail, what she'd managed to overhear on Saturday night, much of which will probably turn out to be irrelevant, except you never know. I haven't really had the chance to sit down and codify everything people have told me, and there are still people I haven't spoken to. But I do remember, she did say something about Caroline Cash, but I was distracted by a phone call, so she never got to impart what it was she wanted to say. I half-expected her to be sitting on the doorstep of the library this morning to continue her revelations."

"Sounds as if she was saving them up for me," said Jenny. "Because I was doing a stint on our reception desk while she was in with Alison having this filling looked at – Alison said it was all a nonsense when she'd gone, just an excuse, and there was nothing wrong at all – so when Annette came out, she was pouring on the sympathy to me, full of concerns that I might have been affected by the sight of the body on Saturday. I told her, I'm made of sterner stuff than that."

"Well, don't spread that around too much," smiled Tania. "Although you weren't exactly calm and collected when you came through here to tell me what had happened. But I've been playing the 'I'm worried about Jenny and I just want to help clear things up to set her mind at rest' card for all I've been worth over the last few days when I've been chatting to people. It's proved surprisingly useful."

"Glad to help," replied Jenny with a laugh.

"So, tell me what Annette had to say," urged Tania. "Did it relate to Carrie? Because I've already talked to her after what you told me about that remark that Professor Kates made to her about the prop diamond necklace in the murder game. Wasn't it supposed to have been stolen by the housekeeper, or some such?"

Jenny shrugged. "It might have been. To tell you the truth, I got a bit confused about all the clues in the game and how they fitted together. I'm not a very good detective, unlike some people I know. But funnily enough, it was something about stolen goods that Annette overheard. According to her, the professor was speaking to Caroline Cash, and it might have been about the necklace in the game, I suppose, but he was talking about stolen goods such as jewellery, and he mentioned about how in court he's often heard evidence about how things are retrieved through tracking down the fence – isn't that what they call someone who handles stolen items?"

"It is indeed. And ...?"

"And apparently, the professor said how amusing it would be if there they were, sitting on the fence at that very moment. What with cash transactions being untraceable. Sounds like a pretty awful pun to me, and it didn't sound as if Caroline was particularly amused, the way Annette tells it. Not that the professor struck me as much of a comedian anyway. So there was that."

"You mean there's more?"

"Oh yes."

"Well, let me just get this last batch of books to put back on the shelves, and you can tell me as I work." Tania collected the final armful of books from the trolley and headed for the Romantic Fiction section, Jenny at her heels. "So what else did Annette have to say?"

"It was about that painter woman, Monica whatshername."

"De Glenn."

"That's the one." Jenny pulled a face. "Silly name. Sounds fake to me. Not real at all. Anyhow, there was something Annette heard, but she said it didn't make any sense to her. I don't know if it will to you."

"Well, come on, let's have it."

"It was just a few words really."

"And they were ...?"

"'Working hand in glove'," concluded Jenny.

"Hand in glove?" echoed Tania. She placed the final volume in its place on the shelving, and rounded the end of the fitment, only to come face-to-face with a silent figure. "Oh!" she uttered in surprise. "Goodness. I didn't know anyone was there. I didn't hear you come in. Hello, Monica."

Monica de Glenn looked Tania and Jenny up and down. "Did I hear my name being taken in vain?"

"Oh no, not at all," said Tania swiftly, covering Jenny's evident embarrassment at being caught indulging in gossip. "We were just chatting about last Saturday night. Reminding ourselves who was there and so on. Wondering what the latest news was."

"I see," said Monica. "Funnily enough, I've been doing much the same thing. I'd heard the rooms in the Town Hall were open to the public once again, and I thought I'd take a look around to see if any thoughts struck me that might help the police with their investigation. And then I remembered there was a book I wanted to consult about Elizabeth Frink's small bronzes, so I popped round to see if I could catch you before you close up."

"Actually, I'm rather glad you did," replied Tania. "I wanted a chat, and there's a few minutes before we close, so now is as good a time as any, if you don't mind. As there's nobody about."

"Not at all," said Monica smoothly, and shot a sideways look at Jenny.

"I'd ... er ... I'd better be getting on anyway," said the nurse awkwardly. "Wouldn't want to be in the way. Bye, Tania and ... er ..." She tailed off, and scuttled for the exit.

"Now," said Tania brightly, as the front door closed behind her assistant, "let's see what we can do about finding that book you were after. Elizabeth Frink, you say. Didn't I see a programme about her work on television not too long ago? *'Fake Or Fortune'*, wasn't it?"

"You may well have done," said Monica carelessly.

"We'd better have a look in the catalogue." Tania seated herself once more at her work station and clicked a few keys on her computer. "And there we are. *'Elizabeth Frink – Sculpture re-imagined'*. And ..." Further clicks. "We have a copy, and it isn't out on loan. Isn't that fortunate? It's just over here in the 'Biographies' section." She led the way to a set of shelves, pulled out a volume, and passed it to Monica. "There. That didn't take too long, did it? Is that what you were after?"

Monica flicked briefly through the pages. "Exactly. Thank you, Tania."

"We'd better get it checked out for you." Back to the desk, and a few seconds work with a scanner. "There. All done." Tania gave a friendly smile. "Do you know, I'd forgotten that you make bronze figures. Is that commissions for the same kind of people who want portraits of their dogs?" A nod. "I expect that must have been quite expensive, setting up all the equipment and so on. But of course, your main activity is painting, isn't it? I've seen those advertisements in the local paper, where you offer to undertake commissions for people's pets."

"Among other things, yes."

"So I gather that must have given you quite a lot in common with poor Professor Kates," suggested

171

Tania.

Monica seemed puzzled. "No," she frowned. "What on earth makes you say that?"

"Oh, did I misunderstand?" queried Tania. "It's just that I was speaking to Alex Blaine, and she was telling me about some of what went on on Saturday before that awful discovery of the professor's body. And one of the things she mentioned was that she happened to be near you when you were having a conversation with the professor, and she overheard him telling you that at one time, in his student days, he had done a fine arts course."

"He may have said something of the kind," said Monica, her tone reserved. "I really can't remember."

"And apparently he went on to say," continued Tania, "that he was particularly interested in the painters of the impressionist period, and he was familiar with their styles. It sounds as if he might have been quite expert on the subject. And I wondered if it might have cropped up in conversation at some time or other at one of your meetings, you both being members of the Literary Society."

"Not that he was a frequent attender," pointed out Monica. "And they weren't that kind of meeting. The subject never arose."

"And yet it seems to have arisen more than once on Saturday night," persisted Tania. "If what I've heard is correct."

"My goodness." Monica gave a tight smile. "There seems to have been an awful lot of eavesdropping going on. I suppose this was another one of Annette Curtin's little tales. I seem to remember she was going around with her ears flapping, as she usually does. Dreadful poisonous woman."

Tania was surprised at the venom in Monica's voice. "Actually, no. It wasn't Annette at all. In fact, several people have told me that Professor Kates had quite a distinctive loud raspy voice, so it would probably be difficult not to overhear what he was saying. But in this case, it happened to be my colleague Jenny. As you know, she was going around with drinks and snacks, carrying out her waitressing duties, and she passed by you and the professor when you were speaking of a particular painting. And funnily enough, it was one of the impressionist ones. There's a work by Sisley next door, isn't there?"

"I believe so." Monica sounded wary.

"Of course, it may have been nothing to do with that particular painting. In fact, it doesn't sound as if it would make a lot of sense. The professor seems to have made some remark about 'oiling the wheels', but Jenny couldn't hear what he was referring to. Maybe something to do with the way in which the gallery was able to acquire the painting?" hazarded Tania.

"I really have no idea what he may have meant," replied Monica shortly.

"But then he apparently went on to talk about 'wielding the oils', as some sort of clever pun. Although from what I can gather, Professor Kates wasn't the type to make jokes. Can you shed any light on what he may have meant?"

"I'm sorry, Tania. I really don't recall the conversation in any detail," declared Monica.

"Perhaps it might jog your memory if we were to pop through and take a look at the painting," suggested Tania. "I've got a key for the pass door into the main Town Hall building. Just let me lock the front door, as it's pretty much closing time, and

173

we can go through."

"Well, if you insist." Monica's reluctance was plain.

Tania darted to the library front door, locked it, and returned to her desk where she collected a fresh bunch of keys. "Here we are," she said, extracting one and unlocking the door which led through to the Town Hall foyer, before leading the way into the gallery. "And there it is. A rural landscape, by Sisley. Ringing any bells?"

"Not a one," responded Monica, displaying very little interest.

"Now here's an interesting thing," remarked Tania, leaning forward to read the notice alongside the painting. "It seems as if I was quite wrong about the acquisition of the painting. It says here that it was discovered by and purchased from an anonymous source with council funds about five years ago. Goodness! That sounds rather mysterious."

"Indeed."

"And they have no idea where or who it came from," marvelled Tania. "No wonder the professor would have been intrigued."

"I dare say we shall never know why," said Monica. "And," she added, as the chimes of the Town Hall clock could be heard striking the half hour high above, "I really ought to be going. Thank you for sorting out the book, Tania."

"Oh, just one or two things before you go," Tania forestalled her. "Because I was wondering if you could help me with regard to the times that people came and went during that crucial period before the body of the professor was discovered. You know, when everyone was upstairs in the mayor's parlour for the main course of the supper. Do you

174

think you can remember anything about people's movements?"

"I couldn't say. I wasn't paying much attention to who did what and when. I didn't realise I'd need to."

"No, of course not," smiled Tania. "Although I'd have thought that an artist such as yourself would need to have quite keen observation. So if I tell you what I've been told, perhaps you might be able to confirm it."

Monica shrugged. "If you think it will help." She didn't sound over-enthusiastic.

"We know that Professor Kates came back downstairs pretty much immediately," began Tania. "He doesn't seem to have been too taken with the food on offer. And then a little while after that, Ivan Ocean and Carrie Cash came down, heading for the smoking shelter outside."

"Oh, I remember that. Somebody made a fuss about smoking indoors."

"Good. And then a little while later, Ellie Dee came down, she says to go to the loo, and you followed her just afterwards."

"Now that I do remember," said Monica. "She vanished into the loo at speed. I wondered if she might be ill. But actually, Ellie wasn't the first down. Now I come to think of it, Jack Hughes was ahead of her. And I noticed that he was heading for the table where the clue items from the murder game were laid out. I assume he wanted to refresh his memory about them. Actually, it's all coming back to me. Because Roland Tighe appeared shortly afterwards, and he must have had the same idea, because I think he headed in the same direction."

"And did you notice the movements of any of

175

these people while you were down in the gallery?" enquired Tania.

"Not really. The smokers were obviously still outside, and I didn't see whether Ellie came out of the loo or not. I did see Jack go off around the gallery just after Roland arrived, so maybe he didn't want to share his ideas with him at that point. And then Roland also moved away, so I thought I'd pick up on their idea and see if a fresh look at the clue items would spark any new thoughts in my mind. After all, we were all still concentrating on the fictional comedy murder at that time. None of us had any idea of what was to come."

"And when you got to the evidence table, did it spark any new thoughts?" asked Tania. "Did you make any startling deductions?"

A smile and a shake of the head. "Sorry, Tania. Nothing." Monica suddenly caught her breath. "Oh! Except ..."

"Except what?"

"When I was looking over the evidence items, I did notice one thing. Or rather, I didn't notice."

"I don't know what you mean."

"That police truncheon," said Monica. "The one that they think was used to kill the professor."

"What about it?"

"It wasn't there."

Chapter 16

As Monica left the Town Hall through the front entrance, leaving Tania still wide-eyed at the revelation, her path crossed with that of Ron Faye, who spotted his wife and made straight for her. "Oh, there you are," he stated with a quizzical look. "I was wondering what was going on. Library front door locked, all the lights on, and no response to my knocking. I thought something might have happened, so I came round to ask at the reception desk here if they knew anything."

"You're right in one way," replied Tania slightly abstractedly, still gathering her wits. "Something has happened." She pulled herself together. "Come with me. We'd better go back through to the library so that I can close up properly." She led the way through the pass door and subsided into her chair at the front desk.

"Well?" said Ron, gazing at his wife. "Don't keep me in suspense. What is it that's happened? Is it anything to do with Monica de Glenn? Because she almost ran over me in the doorway as I was coming in."

"It's very much to do with Monica," said Tania. "Or rather, something she told me."

"I know she was on your list of people to talk to," said Ron, "but I didn't know you'd arranged to meet her here. How did you lure her into the Town Hall? Did you pretend you were seeking her input on the visuals of the scene of the crime, or some other artful device?"

"Nothing of the sort," returned Tania. "In fact, she turned up in the library out of the blue. She wanted a book about a sculptor she was interested in, and I thought the opportunity was too good to miss.

177

Actually, she appeared just as Jenny Chandler had called over after work to impart the latest gossip from Annette Curtin, and it was slightly embarrassing because Jenny mentioned Monica's name, so things didn't start on a particularly promising note."

"But you did have a talk to her? You did manage to touch on some of the things we'd been told by the people you'd already spoken to?"

"Yes. I asked her how close she was to Professor Kates, given what we'd heard about his remarks about painting and so on, but she was adamant that the two of them weren't particularly close. But she also confirmed what people had told us about who went where during that crucial forty-five minutes during which the professor was killed, so we've got a pretty firm timeline of who came downstairs and when. It's not complete, but it's reasonably clear."

"So, can you remember?"

Tania frowned in concentration. "I think so. The exodus from the mayor's parlour started about quarter past nine, when Ivan and Carrie went out for their ciggy break. And they were followed at intervals of a minute or two by, in order, Jack Hughes, Ellie Dee, Monica herself, and Roland Tighe."

"And did she have any information as to who did what and when?" asked Ron.

"She was pretty vague on the subject. And there was certainly no mention of seeing anyone go into the reading room, so no help there."

Ron reflected. "You haven't mentioned Donna McIntosh. Did her name not crop up?"

"No, actually," said Tania. "Nobody's said anything about her so far. We must get around to talking to her. There's bound to be something she's seen or heard."

"I suppose the best way to contact her would be through Alex Blaine," suggested Ron. "She could probably organise something. And of course, there's that other chap from the TV station who was her plus-one at the murder evening."

"Lindsey Doyle?"

"That's the one. Why don't you give Alex a call? No time like the present."

"I will." Tania produced her phone from her handbag and dialled. "Hello, Alex. Tania Faye. Can you talk?"

"Not really. We're about to go on air with Spotlight Today in less that thirty minutes."

"Sorry. I'll be quick." She put the phone on speaker. "It's just that I wanted to have a talk with Donna McIntosh and your friend Lindsey, and I wondered if you would be able to suggest something."

"Hold on a second ... yes, tell the director I'll be there in two seconds ... sorry, Tania. It's a bit hectic here."

"Would it be better another day?"

"Actually, probably not. Lindsey's going off straight after the show to cover a Test Match somewhere up north, and he won't be back for days. Look, can you come over to the studios now? Donna's doing the weather on tonight's show, and Lindsey's in doing a piece about the cricket, so you could catch both of them when we're off-air."

Tania looked up at Ron. "What do you think?"

Ron shrugged. "No problem. There's a casserole at home waiting to be put in the microwave, so we'll just eat a bit later. It sounds like an opportunity not to be missed."

179

"Alex, you're on."

"*Right. Come to Reception by seven and I'll bring you through. And now I really have to go.*"

"Go. See you later." Tania disconnected.

"Right. Sorted. But you still haven't told me what this amazing revelation of Monica's was," pointed out Ron. "So what was so jaw-dropping?"

"You remember when you did that visualisation of what was on the evidence table?"

"One of my finer moments," smiled Ron. "So what about it?"

"And you mentioned the police truncheon which Inspector Bright seems firmly to believe was the murder weapon?"

"Yes?" said Ron, still not seeing Tania's point.

"Well, that's the thing. Monica said that when she went downstairs to look at the clue items, the truncheon wasn't there. It had been removed."

"Wow!" Ron was astonished. "That has to be significant. And yet it was there when we looked at the table after the murder. Has she told the police any of this?"

"She didn't say. I don't think so."

"That means that whoever was at the evidence table before her is right up front on the suspects list. We need to take a closer look at the timeline, and maybe speak to the people ahead of Monica once again."

"Agreed," said Tania. "And speaking of interviewing people, we'd better get a move on if we're going to get to the TV studios in good time." Within a few minutes, library lights switched off and doors firmly locked, the couple were on their way to their car.

*

In mid-journey, Tania's phone unexpectedly rang.

"Hello, Alex. Problem?"

"No, not at all. I was just going to say that, when you get here, head for the gate which leads to our section of the multi-storey car park next to the studios. I've given your name to the chap on the barrier, and he'll buzz you in."

"Thanks, Alex. We'll probably be a bit early. The Westchester rush-hour traffic doesn't seem too bad."

"Fine. See you soon. Gotta go." Click.

The Wessex Radio & TV studios were housed in a striking building just off Westchester's city centre which looked to have pretensions to be considered as a modern cathedral of communication. A soaring glass atrium rising to a point had something of the air of a church steeple, and the sturdy concrete ribs supporting it were reminiscent of flying buttresses. The area surrounding the studios, normally bustling during the day, flanked by a civic park with benches and play areas on one side and, on the other, office buildings whose brightly-lit windows currently showed a total absence of activity, seemed oddly silent and forlorn, now that the business day was done.

Following Alex's instructions, Tania and Ron were soon making their way into the reception area of Wessex TV. A brief exchange with the person manning the desk, a murmur into a microphone, and Alex Blaine burst through the door from the studio area.

"Come with me," she said breathlessly. "I've got exactly fifty-seven seconds to get back to the studio floor."

"I didn't realise you worked on live programmes," said Tania as she and Ron followed Alex's swift progress down the corridor.

"Continuity," explained Alex briefly. "We multi-task around here. Lindsey's finished his piece already. He's in the Green Room. That door there." She pointed. "Gotta go." She disappeared at speed through a heavy door beneath a red light flashing 'ON AIR'.

Tania pushed open the door, to find a cosily-lit room lined with plump sofas, with a table at one end bearing coffee and tea machines, jugs of juice, bowls of fruit, and a rack with an array of cakes and biscuits. Above the table was a large wall-mounted television displaying the programme currently being broadcast, in which a glamorous presenter was displaying a grimly-determined smile while being vigorously marauded by a chihuahua in a pink jumpsuit. And lounging on one of the Green Room's sofas, dressed in cricket whites which showed off his impressive tan to considerable advantage, was Lindsey Doyle. He sprang to his feet as the couple entered.

"Tania! And ... Ron, isn't it?" he greeted them, with his usual dazzling smile which had caused more than one heart beat faster, in hope if not in expectation. He shook hands with the pair, and ran his fingers through the dark blonde hair which contrasted so attractively with his striking blue eyes. "Good to see you again. And under slightly more pleasant circumstances than when we last saw each other on Saturday. Can I get you something to drink?" He gestured to the refreshments.

"No thanks," declined Ron. "We gather you're probably in a hurry."

"Just a bit," smiled Lindsey. "I'm catching a train north later because I'm off to do some cricket coverage, hence the garb. Our director's silly idea –

stupid man. And it's something of a pain, because my husband Rod only got back from a medical conference this morning, so it's been a case of hello and goodbye. Ships that pass in the night, and all that. The glamorous lifestyle of a consultant and a TV personality, eh? But I'm not in that much of a rush, and Alex tells me you want to pick my brains about the events of Saturday in case I happened to have noticed something."

"Well, we did hope," said Tania.

"Not that I haven't had my brains already comprehensively picked by our crime correspondent," said Lindsey. "Mind you, I had to disappoint her. She was most upset to learn that I didn't actually witness the murder, and I wasn't able to regale her with tales of blood-curdling screams and pools of gore. That was the point at which she lost interest. I felt something of a let-down. So, do please sit down." He resumed his place. "What do you hope I can tell you?"

"Bits and pieces really," replied Tania, seating herself on the other sofa, her husband at her side. "Because I know that you and Alex stayed in the mayor's parlour during the supper break, which was when Professor Kates was killed. And we've already established that the only ones who could have been responsible were some of the people in the Literary Society, because no-one else could have had access to the reading room at the relevant time."

"You have been doing your research," remarked Lindsey. "Sure you're not after Alex's job?" he laughed. "And I don't know how helpful I'm going to be, because I'd never clapped eyes on any of these people before Saturday night."

"Which could be good, because you won't have

183

any pre-conceived ideas about them," said Tania. "What I hope is that your reporter's instincts may have picked up on something useful."

"Flattery will get you everywhere," smiled Lindsey. "So, ask away."

"Did you, for instance, notice people's comings and goings from the supper room during that particular forty-five minutes?"

"I remember there was some to-ing and fro-ing," said Lindsey, "but I couldn't put my hand on my heart and give you a sequence of events. I was chatting to Alex most of the time. Oh, except ..."

"Yes?" Tania's eyebrows rose encouragingly.

"It was just that I was talking over the process of the murder game with Alex at one point while we were eating, because so far I don't think either of us had a clue as to who was going to turn out to be the murderer, and I think I said something to the effect that whoever it was that was revealed as being responsible for the death, I was sure that the atmosphere would become electrifying. Positively lethal, I said, joking. And suddenly there was a commotion next to me, and that girl who was playing the weather reporter ... um ..."

"You mean Ellie Dee?"

"That's the one. She suddenly jumped up and scooted off like a scalded cat. She disappeared downstairs as if all the devils of hell were after her. And Alex and I looked at one another as if to say 'What was that all about?'."

"And did you find out?"

Lindsey shrugged. "No. And a little while after that, we had the real murder, which tended to take our minds off anything else."

"What about your own weather reporter?" intervened Ron. "Your colleague here at the TV

184

station."

"Donna? She's in studio at the moment. She's doing the weather slot on tonight's show, and then again on the late bulletin. What about her?"

"We just wondered if you might have noticed her movements during that supper forty-five minutes," explained Tania. "We've got a pretty clear idea of when all the others went downstairs for various reasons, but nobody's mentioned Donna. We think she must have done so, but we don't know when."

Lindsey considered. "I think you're right. Because Alex and I were talking about the suspects in the game, and how well the people were playing their characters – or not, in some cases – and I remember saying to Alex that Donna ought to be able to give a few professional tips to Ellie. But when we looked around for Donna, we couldn't see her. But I really don't know what time that was."

"Not to worry," said Tania. "I expect we can work it out somehow."

"Although ..." said Lindsey slowly. "That reminds me."

"Of what?"

"Something I overheard earlier on in the evening. I can't remember now whether it was at the start when we were all gathering together for the first time, or later on during a break. And I don't suppose it matters much."

"So what did you hear?" enquired Tania.

"It was Professor Kates in conversation with Donna. I say 'in conversation'. If you could call it that. He had something of a lecturing style, from what I heard. And that voice. Like fingernails down a blackboard. There's a man who was never cut out for television."

"And what was it he said?"

"I only tuned in part-way through, but he seemed to be boasting about his intellectual achievements, and he said to Donna 'I reached my position through professional talent, unlike some. Whereas there is a word for people who use other talents to get where they are'. And Donna just looked up at him with those doe eyes of hers and muttered something about having had to work very hard to get her job, and the professor sneered 'I'm sure you did, young lady', and then walked off."

"Interesting," mused Tania. "I don't suppose you overheard any other snippets during the course of the evening?"

"There was one thing I heard in passing, and that was when the professor was speaking to that young student Ivan. Mind you, it sounded as if it could well be something to do with his course work at university, because he seemed to be commenting on his writing style. Professor Kates said that he'd cast an eye over some work that Ivan had produced, and there were what he called 'unaccountable discrepancies'. And I thought, surely that's all a matter of taste. Some people don't like the way I present my sports reports, but that doesn't mean there's anything wrong with them. Anyway, I didn't hear what Ivan said in reply."

"Did you happen to witness any more exchanges between the professor and the other guests?" enquired Tania.

"As a matter of fact, I did," answered Lindsey, now warming to his task. "And now I come to think of it, it sounded quite intriguing. Not that I'm up on legal matters."

"Legal matters?" Tania sounded quite surprised. "This has to be Professor Kates with his judge's wig on."

"I'm not sure he was actually a judge, love," pointed out Ron. "I think he was just a magistrate."

"Still someone you wouldn't want to face from the dock," retorted Tania. "So, Lindsey, what was this about?"

"It was a mention of the Indecent Publications Act that made my ears prick up," said the sports commentator. "Not the sort of thing you expect to hear mentioned at a social gathering. But again, it was that voice of the professor's that you couldn't not hear. And I don't know how it arose, whether he was talking about a case that had come up before him, but he was speaking with that barrister chap Jack Hughes, so it sounded as if they were talking shop. Anyway, the professor was saying that producing some kinds of writing could be a very risky activity – actually, he pronounced it the French way, '*risqué*' – and anyone who indulged in it could do themselves a lot of damage in the eyes of the law. And Jack said something to the effect that he'd never been involved in a case of that kind, and Professor Kates replied that you could never tell what was going to happen in the future. But then I think we were all summoned to take part in the next section of the game, so that put an end to that." Lindsey looked up at the television on the Green Room wall. "And speaking of putting an end to things, there's Donna doing her weather report, which means the programme's almost finished. I shall have to be going if I'm going to grab at least five minutes with Roderick before I have to dash off to catch my train. So, lovely speaking to you. Best of luck with your sleuthing. Alex says you're a whiz. Bye!" In a sudden whirl of white, he was gone.

187

Chapter 17

"More snippets," remarked Ron, as the couple settled back in their seats while the closing credits of the programme rolled on the television screen. "Nothing much to add to your famous timeline, other than the knowledge that Donna absented herself at some point from the supper room, although we don't know when. And that sudden exit of Ellie's seems rather strange. We know she left the parlour, but the scalded cat bit is a little odd. Why, I wonder?"

"Keep wondering," said Tania. "What I find interesting is the fact that neither Ivan Ocean nor Jack Hughes mentioned the little exchanges with Professor Kates which Lindsey told us about."

"Two obvious explanations," responded Ron. "Either they slipped their minds, which seems a bit strange. You'd have thought that the events of Saturday evening would be seared upon their minds. It's not as if there was a great deal of running about and screaming to drive such things from their memory."

"And the other explanation?"

"You know as well as I do, love. They have something to hide, and it relates to what the professor said to them. We're back to what Jenny told us about everyone's reaction to the mention of guilty secrets in the murder game. More wondering, I suspect. And there's the other elephant in the room," added Ron. "Or rather, the elephant that wasn't in the room. If what Monica said is correct, that police truncheon which disappeared and then magically reappeared needs some explanation."

"I think I'm going to have to do some serious

digging," observed Tania. "Just as soon as our roll-call of suspects is complete."

As if on cue, the door of the Green Room opened and Alex Blaine appeared. "And we're off air. How did you get on with Lindsey?"

"Very well, I think," said Tania. "He's given us a few things to think about, so there's just Donna left for us to speak to. Is she with you?"

"No, she's gone back to her dressing room. I didn't have a chance to catch her at the end of the programme, but I can take you along there now. She'll be in no rush – she's doing the late weather report."

"You mean she has to hang about doing nothing for several hours waiting for the late night bulletin?" enquired Ron. "That's a bit of a pain, isn't it?"

"Oh no," smiled Alex. "That one is pre-recorded. But they won't be shooting the VT for a good half-hour, so you should have plenty of time for a chat. Come on through." She led the way along a corridor.

"Does she know we're here?" asked Tania.

"Actually, no. I never got the opportunity to mention that you were coming."

"Well, she'll find out soon enough," said Ron, as he and Tania followed Alex, who stopped at a door and tapped.

"Who is it?" came the voice from inside.

"It's just Alex. Sorry to disturb you, but I've got some visitors for you. I'll leave you two to it," Alex added in a whisper. She pushed open the door, pulled a face as if to say 'Sorry', but then made her escape back towards the studio.

Donna McIntosh's face registered surprise as the couple entered her dressing room. She stood and

189

switched on a welcoming smile, but then her features clouded over as she realised the identity of her visitors. "Oh. I thought it was fans wanting autographs. But it's you, isn't it? You're the ... from the ..."

"That's right, Donna," said Tania in her most soothing tones. "It's Tania Faye from the Ramston Library, and this is my husband Ron. You must remember us from last Saturday night."

"Yes, I do," replied Donna uncertainly. "But why are you here? What do you want with me?"

"We just wanted a chat about what happened," said Tania, deciding to repeat her well-rehearsed excuse regarding her Saturday library assistant. "My friend Jenny – I expect you'll remember her – she was the waitress helping to serve the food and drinks – she works with me in the library, and she was really upset at the thought that one of the people there is a murderer, so I'm trying to find out everything I can so that I can set her mind at rest."

"Oh. I see." Donna seemed to accept the story.

"So do you mind if I ask you a few questions?"

"You'd better sit down." Donna subsided once more into the chair facing her make-up mirror and gestured vaguely towards the small sofa across the room.

"You'll already have spoken to the police, I expect," began Tania.

"Yes, on Saturday."

"But not since?"

"No. I told them everything I know then."

"Ah, well here's the thing, Donna," said Tania. "People don't always remember all the significant facts in the heat of the moment. Sometimes it takes a little while for the mind to clear. And that's what I'm hoping you can help me with."

"Well, I'm not sure ..." Donna seemed uncertain.

"We saw you at the end of tonight's show," said Ron with an apparent abrupt change of tack. "Isn't it funny how television changes people? They do say that the camera makes everyone look ten pounds heavier, but I can't say that it seemed to have any adverse effect on you."

"Ron, I don't really see that this has anything to do with ..." interrupted Tania with a frown.

"In fact, I thought you looked very good on screen," ploughed on Ron. "You know, exuding authority despite the fact that you're quite young. Very professional, I thought." He flicked a sideways look at his wife.

"Yes, absolutely." Tania, with the smallest of smiles, picked up the hint smoothly. "You explained everything very clearly. I suppose that's all a result of the training, isn't it?"

"Oh, the autocue isn't that frightening," said Donna. "And after a while, you don't even notice that the camera's there."

"No, I meant the training as a meteorologist," said Tania. "In fact, I heard that some people at the murder evening were surprised, when the characters were given out, that the part of the TV weather presenter was given to someone else. Ellie, wasn't it? Didn't someone suggest that you ought to be giving her tips about the technicalities of your job?"

"I ... I don't remember that," replied Donna uneasily.

"I'm sure it would have been a great help," insisted Tania. "So, just out of interest, where did you train?"

"Actually, I didn't," admitted Donna after an embarrassed pause. "I started here because

191

someone thought I might do well on screen. A new face on the programme. That was it."

"Oh, I see. Well, that would explain something that's been puzzling me. You see, we've just been having a chat with your colleague Lindsey Doyle, before he had to dash off for this cricket match job of his, and he overheard a remark by Professor Kates when he was talking to you on Saturday. Apparently he said something to the effect that his professional qualifications were among the best, and he was casting doubts on yours. He said something about people getting jobs through other routes."

"Did he?" Donna seemed uncertain how to react. "He may have done, I suppose."

"And now I see what he meant," smiled Tania. "So it was in fact a lucky chance that you're doing what you do. Through a friend, was it?" she asked innocently.

"Something like that," replied Donna.

"And that ties in perfectly with something else that somebody mentioned to me. Honestly, there seems to have been so much chit-chat taking place on Saturday, it's a wonder anyone could make any sense of the conversations going on around them. But the point is, there was one thing that one of your fellow-guests happened to overhear, because I gather that the professor had quite a penetrating voice. He was speaking to you, funnily enough on the same subject that we've just touched on, and apparently he was telling you that he knew one of the directors at the station here, and this friend of his had told him that there were some very interesting promotion processes in place. I don't suppose you can shed any light on what he might have meant?"

192

"Don't they say that in business, it's not what you know, it's who you know?" put in Ron. "I expect it's very much the same in television, eh, Donna?"

"Yes, I suppose so." The Bambi-like blink was back.

"And how well you know them," added Tania. A slight silence fell. "Tell me, Donna, how well did you know Professor Kates?"

"Hardly at all, really. I mean, it's not as if I've been a member of the Literary Society for long. It was Alex Blaine who persuaded me to join, and I'd hardly met the professor before. He didn't come to all the meetings."

"So you wouldn't have any reason to dislike him. Is that what you're saying?"

"No. No, of course not. Why should I?" There was a faint hint of desperation in Donna's voice.

"It's just that, obviously, one of the people present on Saturday must have had a very different view of him. Different enough to wish him serious harm. But not you."

"No," repeated Donna.

"So what we wondered," said Ron, taking up the conversation, "was whether you might have noticed the movements or actions of any of the others which might point in a helpful direction. You see, it all comes down to the forty-five minutes before the body was discovered, when everybody went upstairs to the mayor's parlour for the main course of supper. I assume you did the same?"

"Yes. Everyone did."

"But then we're told that Professor Kates came back downstairs more or less straight afterwards. Evidently what was on offer in terms of refreshments wasn't to his liking. Or perhaps he may have had some other reason for his movements. Would you know anything about that?"

"No," said Donna. "I didn't notice him go. I think everyone was crowding around the food table."

"But then quite a few of the others disappeared back down to the ground floor at odd times for various reasons," resumed Tania. "We've been told about most of them. You know, going outside for a smoke, taking a loo break, checking over the clues in the murder game. But there's one gap in the list. Nobody has mentioned you. So, can you tell us about what you did?"

"Nothing, really. I just had some food."

"So you're saying you stayed up in the mayor's parlour all the time?"

"Yes. Well, no." Donna seemed flustered.

"So, which was it? Did you leave the supper room? And did you see the professor?"

"All right, I did go back down," admitted Donna. "And I did go looking for the professor. I wanted to talk to him."

Tania's eyebrows rose. "What about?"

Donna wriggled uneasily. "Actually, it was about what he'd said to me earlier. You see, I didn't want him going around saying … what he'd said. People might have got the wrong idea about me."

"Indeed," replied Tania drily. "And did you find him?"

"No. I looked around the gallery, but I couldn't see him. And there were people about the place, some of them looking at the clue table, so I wondered if he might have gone through to the reading room, but I couldn't get past them without being noticed. And I didn't want people to see me, so I just came away."

"You didn't get a chance to look at the clue table?"

194

"No. I've said. There were people around it."

"And you didn't go back to look? I just wondered if you might have noticed the police truncheon that was part of the display."

"Why would I? Anyway, there was always someone around."

"So you simply returned upstairs?" Tania sought to confirm.

"Yes. I just sat in a corner and waited, and then the detective called us all together to go back down to the reading room, and that's when we discovered ..." Donna broke off, wide-eyed.

"Which must have come as a great shock to everyone. Including you," sympathised Tania. "Because you'd seen or heard nothing to indicate that any of the others had anything against the professor, or would have any reason to wish him harm?"

"I did see him and Jack Hughes looking daggers at one another at one point," said Donna. "But I have no idea why. And I got the impression that he and Roland Tighe didn't get on too well, but I didn't actually hear either of them say anything."

"Those two again," murmured Ron to Tania. "That's definitely a conversation to be had."

At that point there came a tap at the door, and a young man poked his head into the room. "Donna, they're setting up for the VT for the late-night report. Studio in five, please."

Donna got to her feet. "I have to go. And I need to change first, so if that's all ..."

Tania stood. "Of course. We'll get out of your way. And thank you for your help. What you've told us has given us a great deal to think about. Let's go, Ron. I'm sure we can find our own way out." The couple made their way out of the dressing room and along the corridor towards reception, leaving Donna with a troubled look on her face.

*

"Ruthless murderer giving Professor Kates a vicious whack about the head?" said Ron, as the pair approached their car. "She doesn't seem the type."

"Worms turn," replied Tania darkly. "She might be all fluff and false eyelashes, but you never know what some people will resort to if they find themselves under threat."

"So what's the plan?" Ron held the passenger door for Tania and then climbed in on his own side. "Other than head home for a slightly belated supper? Accompanied by a glass of wine – or two – as a well-earned reward for our efforts. Or to be honest, your efforts. I feel much more like the Captain Hastings in this partnership."

"Captain Hastings was a very valuable sounding-board, darling," pointed out Tania as Ron pulled out of the car park and headed for the main road to Ramston. "And you notice things. Like that rubber glove that was there and then wasn't."

"I think much more worrying is the truncheon that was there and then wasn't, and then was there again. You've said that Inspector Bright did all but confirm that it was the murder weapon, without saying so in so many words. And we have a discrepancy. Monica said it was absent, Donna doesn't seem to have any idea, and nobody else has mentioned it, least of all Jack Hughes or Roland Tighe. I'm thinking that you're going to need to speak further to those two."

"That's not necessarily going to be an easy conversation," mused Tania. "We didn't exactly leave Roland on the best of terms, and I have a

196

feeling that Jack is probably going to be tight-lipped."

"You'll worm it out of them," said Ron confidently.

"And then I think I'm going to have to sit down and do some serious research into all our people," said Tania. "Now that we've finally spoken to everyone. The amount of oblique hints that have been dropped here and there, chiefly by Professor Kates, must mean that there's something to be unearthed."

"And you have the entire resources of your library, not to mention the internet, at your disposal. If you can't find something, it's because it isn't there to find. And that," suggested Ron firmly, "is a job for tomorrow. For tonight, your main task is to get your chops around a portion of my finest Devonshire chicken casserole, together with a few glugs of Pouilly Fuissé, which I took the precaution of putting to chill."

"Oh darling, you're so sophisticated," laughed Tania. "But you're the boss when it comes to catering. So, home, James."

*

"I've decided to walk to work again this morning," announced Tania as she put on her coat.

"More thinking time?" enquired Ron, as he loaded cutlery into the dishwasher.

"Partly that. But there's that odd discrepancy about the truncheon nagging at me, and I'd like to try and sort it out. Which means that I need to have another word with Roland Tighe, so I thought I'd pop into his shop as soon as it opens, before he gets busy with customers."

"Hmmm." Ron's expression was sceptical. "On a scale of one to ten, how happy do you think he's

197

going to be if you come asking questions again?"

"About minus three," smiled Tania, "but it has to be done."

"Are you sure you don't want a bodyguard?" asked Ron half-seriously.

"Best not. If we go in mob-handed, I think it's probably going to raise his hackles more than if I talk to him alone. I shall exude sweetness, full of apologies if we managed to offend him on Monday. After all, I'm just asking one question. 'Roland, you're the only one who can help me' – that sort of thing. People are flattered if you throw yourself on their mercy."

Ron gave his wife a look. "You, love, are a dangerous woman when you have your mind set on something. Remind me never to get on the wrong side of you."

"As if you ever could, darling." Tania put her arms around Ron's neck and kissed him lightly on the lips. "Because you know it would be more than your life's worth," she added, laughing.

"So that's one question. And not the only one you're going to be asking, surely. Because Roland isn't the only one who can help, is he?"

"True," agreed Tania. "I have to put the same question to Jack Hughes. Which may or may not depend on Roland's answer, of course. And if he's prepared to re-open our conversation, of course. And if I can reach him, of course."

"And once you've done that ...?"

"Then, circumstances permitting, and if we're not inundated with a flood of borrowers with impossible requests, I shall delegate the running of the place to Susie while I tuck myself away at one of the library's internet stations and see what I can ferret out in terms of background information about all our suspects. It must be possible to make some sort of sense out of what Professor Kates was hinting or implying or whatever it was he was doing. I just wish we'd thought to make notes as we went along talking to people, but it would rather have dented the 'casual conversation' vibe."

"People might not have been so ready to talk," agreed Ron.

"That's why I got up a bit early this morning. I've spent the last hour noting down everything I could remember from what people have said. Three cheers for the habit of memorising lines at the dramatic society."

"You'd better put your Poirot head on then," advised Ron. "Those little grey cells are going to be working overtime. And I'd offer to put my twopenn'orth in, except that I've got a conference call with one of my clients this morning, and I have a horrible feeling that, once he's offloaded all his problems on to me, that's going to tie me to my own computer for the rest of the day."

"You have to earn a living," pointed out Tania. "We can't live off fresh air and a librarian's meagre salary. So you do your stuff, I'll do mine, and we can catch up this evening." A glance at the kitchen clock. "I'd best be on my way." Another quick kiss, and she was heading for the front door.

Chapter 18

Tania's timing was perfect. Roland Tighe's assistant Gabe was just reeling out the shop's awning as Tania rounded the corner and approached the door. "Good morning," she called cheerily as she entered, to find Roland putting trays of meat out in the chiller cabinet which formed the counter.

He looked up as Tania entered. "Oh. Good morning, Mrs Faye," he responded guardedly. "Can I help you?"

"Oh Roland, please – it's still 'Tania', surely? And I'm so sorry if you felt that we parted on bad terms when we last spoke. I really didn't set out to offend you. I was simply trying to make sense of all the odd things people had told me."

"Well, that's all right then," replied Roland gruffly. "We'll say no more about it."

"But there is one thing I must say," said Tania, "and that is how delicious those kidneys were. Now my Ron may be a good cook, but those were absolutely the tenderest I've had in a long time. I'm always telling people how lovely your meat is, and those were no exception. So thank you."

"I always make sure my customers get the best," said Roland, now thoroughly mollified. "My dad taught me that, and his dad before him."

"So it's no wonder that you've got such a wonderful reputation," smiled Tania. "You must be very proud of it." Was there a hint of a hesitation before Roland's 'I certainly am', she wondered. "Now, I'm so glad we've cleared the air," she continued, "so that I don't mind asking just one more question about last Saturday night. And it's nothing to do with you, really," she added hastily as

200

a frown began to form on Roland's face. "No, it's really about something I've been told which has been baffling me. And to be honest, you're the only person I know who could help me."

"Oh?" Roland looked puzzled. "What would that be?"

"It was something from the murder mystery game," explained Tania. "I think you went downstairs to the art gallery during the supper break, because that's where the so-called evidence table was, with the clue items."

"That's right. I did."

"Now between you and me," Tania looked around in a somewhat theatrical manner and lowered her voice, "that detective inspector – the real one, not the chap in the game – has more or less confirmed to me that the weapon that killed Professor Kates was the police truncheon. Now that truncheon was on the table when Ron and I looked at it after the police had arrived – Ron has a brilliant visual memory, and he's sure of it. Which means that it had been taken, used in the murder, and then put back. Do you see?"

"Yes," said Roland. "But why does that involve me?" The guarded tone was back in his voice.

"Because one of the people who looked at the table before the professor's body was discovered has stated that, when they looked, the truncheon was gone. And the question is, when did that happen? And since I know that you visited the table, I hoped you could say whether the truncheon was still in place or not when you did."

Roland appeared to consider, his eyes closed. He shrugged. "I can't say. Not that I was there long. I think there was somebody breathing down my neck, so I just got out of the way. I hate being crowded. I think it was there, but I'm not sure. I don't suppose that helps."

"Oh well, it was only a thought," said Tania lightly. "I'll just have to see what I can find out from other sources. Don't worry about it. And now I'd better be getting on, or else I shall be late opening up. But I'll be sure to let you know if I get any more information." She made her way out of the shop, but not before she'd registered the look of uncertainly on Roland's face. 'What sort of answer was that?' she thought to herself. 'No answer at all. And that means ... I have no idea.' With a shake of her head, Tania turned into the Market Square and fumbled in her handbag for the library keys.

*

"Can I beg a favour, Susie?" asked Tania, as she and her assistant were preparing to open up, and Susie was about to wheel the full trolley of returned volumes down the library to replace the books in their rightful places on the shelves.

"Of course," replied Susie. "Anything. Within reason. Just don't ask me for money. I've just had the gas bill."

"Don't worry," smiled Tania. "It's nothing like that. It's just that I want to do a whole heap of research which really can't wait, and I know if I'm sat here at the desk I'm going to be interrupted every five minutes with phone calls and silly questions. If you can take over the desk for me, I can go and hide myself away in the corner at one of the internet stations and get on with things."

"No problem," said Susie, her eyes gleaming with interest. "Is it to do with your investigations into the murder? I bet it is."

"You're just like Jenny," chuckled Tania. "She's always obsessed with wanting to know what progress I'm making when I'm caught up in a murder case. Which seems to be happening with rather depressing frequency," she added, shaking her head.

"I'll get these books back, and then I'm all yours. Give me five minutes."

"That's fine. I've got to make a phone call anyway." As Susie disappeared towards the far end of the library, Tania lifted the receiver.

"Good morning. Putnam Hinder Cage and Lockett."

"Good morning. I wonder, is it possible to speak to Mr Hughes?"

"I'm sorry, Mr Hughes is in court today. May I put you through to someone else?"

"No, it was Mr Hughes I needed to speak to. Will he be back later?"

"I'm afraid I really couldn't say. May I take a message?"

"Could you perhaps ask him if he would contact Mrs Faye at Ramston Library?"

"In connection with what, may I say?"

"Oh, I think he'll know. Do you have any idea when he'll get the message?"

"I'm afraid not. He does happen to be involved in a rather important case," came the prim reply.

"Well, thank you anyway. I'll leave it with you." With a small sigh of frustration, Tania rang off.

"All done," announced Susie, returning to the front desk. "Off you go. I'm in charge now." With a satisfied smile, she settled herself in Tania's place, just as the front door of the library opened to admit the first customer of the day.

Tania headed for the furthest corner of the room where one of the internet stations was located in a quiet alcove, and pulled her notebook from her bag. 'Why on earth was Russell Kates going around on Saturday making pointed remarks to the people at the murder evening?' she wondered, not for the first time. 'What did he hope to achieve? A demonstration of his power over them? Whatever it was, it certainly produced a result he could never have anticipated. I just have to look closely at everything he said to everyone. And I suppose alphabetical order by surname is as good as anything,' she said to herself, pulling out her notebook. 'Being a librarian. So, we'll start with Caroline Cash What do we know about her?'.

Tania had no inkling with regard to Caroline's personal history. She only really knew of her in a business context, that of an antiques dealer, handling jewellery among other things. And jewellery was what seemed to have provoked Professor Kates's comments when the subject arose of the alleged diamond necklace in the murder game. The professor had made mention of instances of stolen jewels – had he been speaking about cases which had come before him in court, or at least cases he'd read about in legal records? Tania swiftly clicked on to the archives of the Wessex County Court, and in addition the files relating to the magistrates courts for the area, but could find no mention of Caroline Cash. That would have been too simple, she mused. But there was Caroline's statement, delivered in haste it seemed, that she would never touch stolen diamond necklaces as they would be far too traceable. Did this sound like the lady protesting too much? What about the reference to fences? And untraceable cash payments? Had the professor seen material which had never actually come to court, but which hinted at dangerous revelations? Did he hit too close to the gold for his own good?

Then there was Ellie Dee. She seemed such a pleasant girl, and had certainly proved highly efficient when carrying out the small electrical job which Ron had invented as an excuse to interview her. So what could account for her jumpiness when there was mention of incompetence? An innocent reference in conversation on Saturday night to sparks flying under certain circumstances, and an electrifying atmosphere, seemed to have spooked her to an unaccountable degree. Professor Kates had apparently referred to some old newspaper records, but he didn't seem to have been specific. Was there an explanation there? Tania brought up on screen the news files of the local and county newspapers in turn, but a search for the name of Ellie Dee produced no results, other than simple listings of advertisements for her business. But ... the professor had spoken of odd coincidences of names. Dawson, he'd said. Tania refreshed her search parameters, and suddenly, there it was. A case a few years before where the entire family of an electrician called Eleanor Dawson had perished in an overnight electrical house fire, leaving her an orphan. Forensic investigation was unable to assign specific blame. Was this what Kates had uncovered? And would the threat of his spreading this knowledge offer to destroy Ellie's life and career?

On to Monica de Glenn. Here was another woman with her own business and a reputation to protect. But how could Professor Kates be in a position to threaten that? He had flaunted his knowledge of art. He had made mention of having studied fine art as a student, and boasted of his knowledge of certain artists' styles. There was that conversation he had had with Monica when in front of the work

205

by Alfred Sisley, one of the Ramston Art Gallery's more mysterious acquisitions. He didn't appear to think much of it, if what he seems to have said about it leaving a bad impression was anything to go by. Had he by any chance encountered any of Monica's pictures at some time, and was he making a similarly dismissive judgement as to her work? Surely not – he was in fact heard to make complimentary reference to her skills. He spoke of oiling the wheels and wielding the oils, which sounded more like admiration for the way she made a living. So what threat could he represent? Where could there be a motive for her to wish him harm?

Who was next on the list? Ah – Jack Hughes. It was irritating not having been able to contact him this morning, but with luck he would be in touch soon. And if not, might that be a black mark against him? Tania reserved judgement for now. But it occurred to her that Jack did not seem to be the most obvious person to be a member of a literary society, especially since he did not appear to be attempting to produce anything in the way of writing. In fact, he had seemed oddly evasive on the subject. So where did Professor Kates's remarks regarding clients for a particular style of reading matter originate? Careers could be enhanced if knowledge of certain powerful people's reading habits were used to influence them? Did that sound oddly like blackmail? And if so, of whom, and by whom? Why was there mention of Indecent Publications? What was the activity that was risky? Or, as Kates had pronounced it in the French way, *risqué*? A sudden inspiration struck Tania, and she turned once more to her search engine. The result was intriguing. In one of the murkier corners of the web she discovered a publication, described as 'Erotic material catering for the discerning gentleman', by an individual named Rhys Kaye. There was no further author information. But could it really be that the barrister was disguising his literary output? And if word were to spread, what would that do to his professional reputation?

Then there was Donna McIntosh to consider. The professor's potential hold over her seemed almost too obvious. Donna herself admitted, albeit slightly reluctantly, that she had no professional qualifications for her job. By contrast, Professor Kates had made great boast to her of his own academic pedigree, to the extent that he seemed almost to be taking a delight in rubbing Donna's nose in it. And he'd also been quite happy to state that, being acquainted with one of the directors of the television company, he was also well aware that not everyone rose up the career ladder by their talents alone. An interesting promotion process, he had called it, which to Tania's ears sounded like nothing so much as the old casting couch. Had Donna in truth sold her favours to get where she was? And would public knowledge of that fact destroy her youthful and wholesome image? She created the impression of a sweet and harmless girl. Could such a person wield a police truncheon to such devastating effect? As Tania had remarked to Ron, 'worms turn'.

As Tania moved down her list, she arrived at Ivan Ocean. A young student with his life ahead of him, perhaps on the first steps of a promising career. He already held posts of considerable responsibility in the Camford University Students Union, but did this fact contain the seeds of his potential

207

downfall? Professor Kates had referred to unaccountable discrepancies in work Ivan had produced. The obvious and superficial explanation was that this might refer to the writing style of the student's academic work, except that the two individuals were not closely linked through Ivan's course. What then? The young man's other chief function was as custodian of the finances of the Students Union, and Kates had spoken of interesting revelations. Had word reached his ear that some student funds had been misappropriated? A swift trawl through the internet made reference to stories of the purchase, at considerable cost, of academic papers from outside sources which were passed off as a student's own work. Could Ivan have been involved in such a scheme? If so, revelation of the fact could blight his prospects irrevocably.

And that just left Roland Tighe. What did Tania know about him? Quite a lot, on the face of it. She and Ron had been customers of his for a considerable period of time, and while not close friends, had always found him affable and pleasant to deal with. That was, until the uncomfortable conversation of a couple of days ago. That showed an aspect of Roland's personality which Tania had not encountered before. How much, she wondered, was this to do with the exchanges which had occurred between Roland and Professor Kates at the murder evening? Surely there was a link, and did it have to do with the professor's apparent propensity for digging back through old records? Historic cases were spoken of. There was even talk of a conviction. Back to the internet went Tania, but her searches brought up no hint of Roland ever having fallen foul of the law. And yet ... here in an old wartime newspaper report was mention of a local butcher who had been investigated for trading in suspected unfit meat during rationing. The investigation had been inconclusive, and the shopkeeper was not named, but was it stretching coincidence too far to imagine that the Tighe family's business might be the one concerned? Roland was evidently proud of his family's long-earned reputation. If the professor had learned something which jeopardised that, might Roland have taken drastic action to preserve it?

Tania sat back and cast her eye once more over her notes. Means, motive, and opportunity – they were all there. The means – without an official declaration by Inspector Bright, it was not absolutely certain that it was a blow from the antique police truncheon which had brought about Professor Kates's death, but Tania was as sure as she could be that there was no doubt on the subject. As to opportunity, the evidence of the various witnesses present had given a fairly clear picture, and the seven people on Tania's list could all have been in the right place at the right time. Unfortunately, there were no conclusive sightings which could rule anyone out or in. And her current exercise proved that all those suspects could have had a motive to wish the professor harm. True, some were stronger than others, but who knew what tiny factor might cause someone to take precipitate action? That was that, then. Apart from the one niggling omission. Could Jack Hughes provide a crucial missing piece of evidence regarding the truncheon? Tania's failure to speak to him again was frustrating.

As if in answer to an unspoken prayer, Susie's head appeared around the corner of the adjacent stack of bookshelves. "I know you didn't want to be interrupted," she said, "but there's a phone call for you. A Mr Hughes – he says he's returning your call. I hope you don't mind. It sounded important."

Tania jumped to her feet. "It could be. Thanks, Susie." She hurried to the front desk and picked up the phone. "Mr Hughes. Thank you for getting back to me."

"To be frank, Mrs Faye, I'm not sure why I did. Other than in the hope that we might be able to bring our conversations to a conclusion. And I hope that this will not take long. The judge has called a brief recess, and I have to be back in court shortly."

"Just a few moments, Mr Hughes," Tania reassured him. "I have just one question."

"Go ahead."

"Towards the end of the supper break on Saturday, I'm told you visited the evidence table to examine the clue items. And I know that you would probably be an expert in considering evidence. My question is, was the police truncheon present on the table at that time?"

There was a few moments' pause. *"I couldn't swear to it absolutely, Mrs Faye, but I believe it was. Is that all?"*

"Thank you so much, Mr Hughes. That is exactly what I wanted to know. I'll let you get back."

A curt 'goodbye', and Jack was gone, leaving Tania listening to the burr of the dialling tone. She gave a small sigh of relief. Was that, she asked herself, the final piece of the jigsaw?

Chapter 19

It was just after five o'clock when Tania looked up from her desk to see Jenny Chandler entering from the street. She had decided to put all her musings on hold in order to talk them through with Ron at leisure during the evening, and had taken over from a clearly relieved Susie, who had not particularly enjoyed the responsibility of fielding the afternoon's range of awkward questions and complicated requests which were normally Tania's domain.

"Hello, Tania," Jenny greeted her. "What's the news? How's the investigation coming?"

Tania gave a small non-committal shrug. "Slowly and steadily. I've finally managed to speak to everyone who was there on Saturday, so Ron and I are going to see what sense we can make of it all this evening."

"Oh good. I can't wait to hear what you think."

"You're really quite invested in this case, aren't you, Jenny?" remarked Tania with an indulgent smile.

"Of course I am," replied the dental nurse. "Why wouldn't I be? After all, it's the first murder I've been involved in. It's a bit exciting."

"Hmmm." Tania did not sound so sure. "Well, don't get too involved. It's probably best to leave it to the professionals."

"Like you?" laughed Jenny. "That'll be the day. Anyway, I came to tell you a little bit of news of my own. They took away the police tape from the special exhibition area in the art gallery this afternoon. Apparently the forensic people have finished in there. They must think there's nothing to find, but I'm not so sure, so I thought I'd go and have a look round on my own."

"I'm sure the SOCO people know what they're doing," declared Tania.

"You never know," said Jenny. "So I'm going to see for myself. And when I find the final clue that they've missed, I'll come back and tell you," she finished triumphantly. "So is it all right if I go through the pass door?"

"Go on then," smiled Tania. "I look forward to hearing about your amazing discoveries." She reached into her desk drawer and handed over the pass door key. "I'm keeping it locked these days. Just drop that back before we close at half past."

"Will do," carolled Jenny, and vanished through the door into the Town Hall main building.

It was some twenty minutes later that Ron arrived in the library, just as Susie was ushering the last borrowers of the day out through the front door. "Ready, love?" he enquired, as the two librarians gathered up their bits and pieces and exchanged farewells as Susie departed.

"Almost," replied Tania. "I'm just waiting for Jenny to drop the pass door key back. She's doing a little sleuthing of her own in the art gallery next door. I'll check how she's getting on." She tried the door. "Oh. It's locked. She must have locked it behind her." A sigh. "No matter. I'll lock up here, and then we can go round and in through the Town Hall front door." All done, she and Ron made their way around to the Town Hall main entrance, passed through the empty foyer, and entered the gallery.

"Well, where is she?" queried Ron.

"She said she was going to take a look at the special exhibition area, now that the police have cleared it." Tania made for the exhibition alcove.

"No sign of her." She circled the central stand on which the 'Kitchen Sink Drama' artwork was displayed, and came to a sudden horrified halt. There, slumped behind the stand, a wicked-looking kitchen knife protruding from her back, lay the huddled body of Jenny Chandler. "Oh no!" She fell to her knees and placed a hand on the body, to be rewarded with a fain moan. "Oh, thank heavens. Ron, it's Jenny! She's been stabbed, but she's alive! For goodness' sake, call an ambulance! Quickly!"

*

The figure propped up in the hospital bed attempted a wan smile as Tania and Ron entered the side room of the top floor ward of Ramston Memorial Hospital.

"Thank goodness," breathed Tania, as she deposited a large bunch of flowers on the foot of the bed. "How are you feeling, Jen?"

The smile grew stronger. "Actually, a lot better than last night," replied Jenny. "They seem to have patched me up pretty well, so now it only hurts when I laugh." A wince to prove the point. "The doctor says I was very lucky. The knife could have caused serious damage, but apparently it hit the shoulder-blade and skidded sideways. An inch in the other direction and it might have been a different story. But now I'm full of painkillers, so feel free to tell me a joke."

"Don't you dare, Ron," warned Tania. "We're just pleased that you're okay, Jen. Because for a horrible moment ..."

"I know," said Jenny, her face solemn. "As you say, for a horrible moment ..."

"So what happened?" enquired Tania. "There was so much rushing around after we found you, and you were in no state to say anything. Can you

213

remember what happened?"

"I did what I told you I was going to do," recalled Jenny. "I went through to the art gallery ..."

"Why did you lock the pass door behind you?" butted in Ron. "Tania and I couldn't get through."

"I didn't," said Jenny. "Somebody else must have turned the ... oh!" Her eyes widened in realisation. "It must have been ..." Her lip trembled for a moment, before she took a deep breath, winced once more, and continued. "Anyway, I started to look round the special exhibition area which the police had just cleared. And I couldn't see anything at first, but then I just noticed a flash of something yellow jammed down behind one of the radiators. I was just going to take a closer look, when I felt a sudden awful pain in my back, and I think I must have passed out from the shock. And that's all really."

"You had no warning? You didn't see or hear anyone?"

"That, Mrs Faye, is one of the questions I was about to ask." The remark came from Detective Inspector Marion Bright who, accompanied by Sergeant Miner, had entered the room unnoticed. "So, Miss Chandler, what's the answer?"

"Sorry, inspector," replied Jenny. "Not a thing."

"But surely it can only be one of the people involved in Professor Kates's murder, inspector," suggested Tania. "Isn't that the obvious conclusion? Although why on earth they should attack Jenny ...?"

"Another question we shall be giving considerable thought to, Mrs Faye," said Bright.

"And you must have been able to eliminate some of the ... am I allowed to call them suspects?"

"Let's call them persons of interest, Mrs Faye."

214

"Because some of them wouldn't have been in Ramston at the time, would they?" continued Tania. "Obviously several of them are Ramston-based, so I should think you'd be looking at them first. But what about the others? For instance, I know that Jack Hughes couldn't have done it because he was tied up in court yesterday afternoon. I spoke to him myself."

"That's as may be, Mrs Faye, but unfortunately, according to my information, the judge in that case called an early adjournment. And Mr Hughes lives in Ramston, so I'm afraid your theory falls to the ground."

"What about Donna McIntosh? She must have been at the studios in Westchester for her weather report on 'Spotlight Today'. Or Ivan Ocean? He's at Camford University."

"Miss McIntosh wasn't due into work yesterday. And Mr Ocean is still residing with his parents. We do check on these things, Mrs Faye," pointed out the inspector drily. "And by the way, speaking of work, I'm surprised to find you here. Don't you have a library to run?"

"We close on Thursday mornings," said Tania. "But what about the case?" she persisted. "You'll be checking on people's alibis, won't you?"

"Please, Mrs Faye, leave us to do our job," insisted Bright. "We do have some experience in these matters. Whereas you, and particularly Miss Chandler here, have discovered the perils of becoming involved in a murder case. You may have acquired a local reputation as a solver of crimes, but now you see how dangerous that can be. Do not allow yourself to be thought of as some sort of detective. It creates a false impression." Tania suddenly caught her breath. "What?"

215

For a moment, Tania didn't speak. She seemed far away. But then she came back into focus. "Just something that struck me, inspector. Perhaps a key fact. But I need to think it through."

"Then do it at home, if you wouldn't mind, Mrs Faye. Mr Faye, do you suppose you can persuade your wife to do that?"

"You should probably have a chat with your colleague Inspector Copper on the subject of persuading Tania to keep clear," replied Ron with a wry smile. "But I'll see what I can do. Come on, love. Let's leave these officers to get on with their work, and we'll adjourn to the Cross Keys for a relaxing drink." He took his wife's arm, and the couple made their way out of the ward.

*

"I must be mad," said Detective Inspector Marion Bright, as she and Sergeant Miner stood in the silent library, deserted but for themselves, Tania and Ron. "I hope this isn't going to be a Saturday evening wasted."

"But if you can't find anything concrete to base a case on, isn't this one way to resolve matters?" enquired Tania.

"Not the normal way," grated an unconvinced Bright.

"And I admit that all I've offered you is deductions based on what I've heard. Nothing solid and factual. And you don't have fingerprint evidence," continued Tania. "You said that you'd not managed to identify anything?"

"A tiny partial, nothing more. Nowhere near enough for a jury to convict."

"But there's no need to go into fine detail about that, is there?" observed Tania. "Mention that you'd discovered a print could be enough to provoke an

216

admission."

"We'll see," grunted the inspector.

"So should we go through?" suggested Tania. "Fortunately, I have a duplicate key." She unlocked the pass door, and the group entered the art gallery.

*

"Thank you all for coming," Alex Blaine had said a little while before, as the group settled themselves into their previous places around the table in the Town Hall's former reading room. Almost everyone from the last Saturday evening was present, with one particularly glaring omission, and the empty and silent chair formerly occupied by Russell Kates provided a mute witness to the events of seven days earlier.

When Tania had first approached Alex on Friday morning with the suggestion to call the meeting, the researcher had at first been reluctant, fearing that such an event would feel bizarre and uncomfortable. However, Tania's persuasive talents, together with the fact that the librarian had managed to win over a wholly sceptic Inspector Bright that the process, given the information she laid out before him, could produce a result, had finally convinced her.

"I know that it may feel odd," Alex continued, "but as Secretary of the Ramston Literary Society, I felt we should do something to commemorate our late Patron and President, rather than continuing to our next normal meeting as if nothing had happened. So I thought a few moments of quiet reflection in the place where he passed, and perhaps a few words from everyone, would be a fitting tribute." There was a mixture of reluctant nods and speculative glances around the table. "So perhaps it would be best to begin with ..." Her voice faded away as the door from the art gallery opened to admit Tania, followed by her husband and the pair of detectives.

"I'm sorry to interrupt proceedings," apologised Tania, "because I understand that you have all been called together with a view to commemorating the late Professor Russell Kates. But it occurred to me that the best way to commemorate the professor would be to bring the case to a conclusion by identifying his murderer."

The speculative looks were renewed, together with some murmurs of protest.

"Whose idea was this?" objected Jack Hughes. "I do hope, Detective Inspector, that you haven't staged this event as some sort of quasi-judicial procedure. Because if that's the case, I strongly object. I thought seriously about not attending in the first place. In fact, I think it would be altogether better if this entire rigmarole was brought to an end." He pushed back his chair.

"Nothing of the kind, Mr Hughes," responded Marion Bright mildly. "There is nothing official about what is happening here. At present," she added. "But Mrs Faye here has convinced me that it might be helpful if everyone were given the opportunity to consider the facts surrounding Professor Kates's unfortunate death. And if one of the parties involved were to absent themselves, that might be considered as indicative of ... something significant, shall we say?"

"As you wish." Jack resumed his seat with evident reluctance. "Well, what form is this 'consideration' supposed to take?"

"I shell leave it to Mrs Faye to explain," said the inspector, and stepped back.

218

Tania cleared her throat. Why was she feeling nervous, she wondered. It wasn't as if this was a novel experience for her. But how could it be easy when people she knew were among those involved? She took a deep breath and began.

"If it weren't an unfortunate play on words, it could be said that Professor Kates was the author of his own misfortune. Not that he was a writer in the context of the Ramston Literary Society, of course. Writing was something that several of the other members indulged in. But it was his utterances which prompted last Saturday's murder. Because the professor had three notable traits. The first was his apparent fondness for discovering, by accident or design, facts about people which they, for varying reasons, might wish to suppress. The second, arising from this, was his habit of using these facts as a weapon to demonstrate his potential hold over those people. And the third was, as I've had described to me by many of you, his distinctive and penetrating voice with which he expressed his knowledge. I was told that, at an early stage in the evening, the person playing the detective who was in charge of proceedings made a statement that 'everyone has a guilty secret'. A simple enough remark when speaking of the game which was about to unfold – but the reaction which followed, though brief, was proof that he was too close for comfort to some of those present. And for one of you, the secret was too dangerous to be allowed to become known.

"I've had many of the snippets of conversation between the professor and several of you relayed to me. The conversations were fragmentary. The professor's implications were by no means clear. But I have resources of my own to draw upon.

Nothing secret or privileged – Inspector Bright here will confirm that I've had no access to restricted police records. In fact, she has done everything she could to dissuade me from involving myself in the case." A dry smile from the inspector in the background. "But in a sense, this is *my* library," continued Tania. "And I cannot help feeling a responsibility for what takes place here, odd though that may seem. And my researches have led me to what I believe to be the facts of the case."

"This may be all very interesting to you, Tania," spoke up Caroline Cash. "But you haven't actually told us anything yet. It's all so much waffle. Is anybody going to explain what we're all doing here? What are these supposed guilty secrets you're talking about?"

Tania coloured slightly. "I'm sorry if I'm being long-winded. I was simply trying to explain some thought processes. But if you wish, I'll be more specific." She looked around the table. "So, perhaps I could begin with the ladies. Donna McIntosh, for instance."

"Me?" exclaimed a startled Donna. "What about me?"

"As guilty secrets go," said Tania, "there are many worse. Professor Kates was heard to speak to you on the subject of the somewhat meteoric rise in your television career. He speculated that, from what he'd heard from his contacts, that rise had not been entirely as a result of your knowledge and talents. Or perhaps, not professional talents. Personal talents, perhaps – a talent for demonstrating your gratitude in a personal way to somebody who could advance your prospects. Not that you would be the first young woman who has

220

trodden that path to success, and I have no definite evidence that it happened in your case, but your reactions to the professor's words, and to our own conversations, hint strongly that he had the rights of it. But concealment of such uncomfortable facts as a motive for murder? As I say, that path is a well-trodden one. Perhaps a cause of a few brief headlines in the tabloids, but murder? It doesn't seem likely to me."

Donna, who had begun to blush ever more as Tania continued, gazed firmly at the hands twisting in embarrassed fashion in her lap and said nothing.

"Let's turn to Ellie Dee." The electrician's head rose, but she remained silent. "It seems that everyone speaks well of Ellie, and deservedly so. Comments on her website are unfailingly positive. She has even carried out a small job in my own house, very satisfactorily, I may say. So why would Professor Kates be going after her? Not because she had produced incompetent work for him, I think. So why the reference to incompetence in his comments to her. And what did he mean when he spoke of an odd coincidence of names? Again, newspaper files from a few years ago provided the likely answer. A young woman – an electrician named Eleanor Dawson – was investigated after an electrical fire in the family home had led to the death of her entire family. Blame was never assigned, but it seems unlikely that Eleanor would ever be able to escape the pointed fingers and the murmured speculation. But a move to a fresh location, and a subtle change of name, might give her a new start. And could well have done, but for the sharp eyes and forensic deductions of a university professor with a nose for embarrassing facts. Would the word go round again, 'No smoke without fire'? Even though Ellie had done nothing wrong. Was her career jeopardised? Was that enough reason to kill a man?

"Shall we consider Monica de Glenn next?" suggested Tania. "Here the motivation seems even more tenuous. She and Professor Kates were overheard discussing one of the paintings in the art gallery, an impressionist work. It seems that the professor was not over-impressed with the artwork, and appears to have made disparaging remarks about it." A small smile. "I suspect that there isn't a creative person, be they writer, painter, or any other art form, who hasn't received criticism at some time or another. And can we seriously suppose that an artist would resort to murder, simply because some philistine, as they would doubtless see it, dared to criticise their style of work? That theory would surely never hold water."

Monica gave Tania a long level look but said nothing.

"So now we'll come on to Caroline Cash, since she was the one who wanted me to talk about specifics. As I understand it, there was an interesting congruence between her own business as an antique dealer and her rôle in the murder game as a jeweller. Indeed, Professor Kates remarked on it. And part of the game revolved around a supposed diamond necklace, stolen during the proceedings. The professor made pointed remarks on the subject, saying what an advantageous position someone like Caroline would be in when handling stolen items. He spoke of such a person, a receiver of stolen goods, as a 'fence', the underworld term. Was he uncomfortably close to the truth? I have to say that there is no trace in any court reports that I

222

can find of Caroline being suspected of receiving stolen goods, but did she give herself away with an unguarded remark when she asserted that she would never touch such items as the purported diamond necklace, since they would be too easy to trace? Being caught engaging in such activity might very well lead to a prison sentence, and that would be a danger which could provoke someone to take extreme action. Lethal violence, perhaps."

Chapter 20

"What's this, Caroline? No denials?" challenged Roland Tighe. "You kicked off this rigmarole, but you don't seem so vocal when things are pointed in your direction."

"Say what you like, Roland," retorted Caroline. "I wonder what we're going to hear about you. But I've got nothing to hide. Have I ever been charged with anything? No. Have I ever even been in court? No. So if there's evidence against me, why doesn't the inspector arrest me here and now?" She glared defiantly at the detective.

A quiet smile crossed the features of Marion Bright. "An interesting suggestion, Miss Cash. But if I were you, I wouldn't be too confident of my situation. Mrs Faye tells us that she couldn't find any reference to you in the records of the court. That may be true. But that doesn't mean that your name is unknown in police files. Questions have been raised in the past. There will perhaps be more in the future. And if Professor Kates was able to voice suspicions, maybe we will be able to answer those questions in a way that you wouldn't appreciate. But for the moment, I'm happy for Mrs Faye to continue to develop her very interesting argument."

"Thank you, inspector," said Tania. "And on the subject of courts, perhaps we ought next to take a look at Jack Hughes. A prominent barrister – a King's Counsel, no less. That's a very highly regarded status, well worth protecting. So when somebody with connections in legal circles says that he has heard implications that that status may have been achieved through questionable means, it's worth taking a closer look. There were two aspects to Professor Kates's hints. Did Jack Hughes know, for example, that a highly-placed individual with the power to advance careers in the law had a fondness for literature of a – shall we say 'adult' nature? However many shades of whatever colour? Not that there's anything illegal in reading such material, as long as the topic does not contravene the law. But consider how the tabloids love to publish tales of judges caught in embarrassing situations. Such a person might use their influence to protect what Shakespeare calls 'the bubble reputation'. A bubble easily popped. Might a barrister, for instance, use their knowledge to persuade this person to assist them? But the reputation of this assumed person was not the only one at risk. What if the author of such material, described by the professor as '*risqué*', were identified? What if they published under the name of Rhys Kaye, and the professor had learned this? Gossip among the legal community probably spreads just as fast as anywhere else, and the prospect of sideways looks and smirks from his colleagues might prove devastating to a barrister's reputation and prospects. To prevent such revelations, perhaps by violent action, could be seen as one way out."

Jack Hughes stood. His face was an impassive mask. "I have no comment on these allegations, save to say that I have done nothing illegal. And the validity of these proceedings is highly questionable, and I shall be bringing the matter to the attention of your superiors, Inspector Bright. Other than that, I have nothing to say, so I shall be leaving."

"Please sit back down, Mr Hughes," said the inspector with a steely smile. "There is nothing official happening here. We are merely listening to the musings of a highly intelligent woman who has been considering a matter which touches her closely."

Tania shot a surprised look in Bright's direction, before resuming at a nod from the detective.

"Caroline Cash says that she was interested to hear what was to be said about Roland Tighe, so let me satisfy her curiosity. Roland is another one who was on the receiving end of Professor Kates's pointed remarks. 'Dead meat' – 'meat on the bones' – the professor seems to have been giving full rein to his fondness for bad puns. But what was behind them? There has never been a hint that Roland has ever been involved in anything questionable. His personal reputation, and that of his shop, is of the highest. Back we go to the professor's fondness for delving through the archives. And there he would have found, by accident or design, the story of a butcher who, during wartime, was on the receiving end of accusations that he had been passing off unfit meat as suitable for human consumption, although the case was never proved. I found the story without difficulty, and it was not hard to guess the identity of the butcher. There was only one long-standing family firm in Ramston which fitted the bill, and rumour can be deeply harmful to a business's success. Roland is a powerful individual. Would a man who can swing a cleaver to dismember a carcase baulk at swinging an antique truncheon in defence of his father's reputation?"

"If I had wanted to have it out with Kates," growled Roland, "I wouldn't have gone sneaking about behind the scenes. I would have knocked the old swine down in broad daylight. It was only the fact that he was so much older than me that saved him."

"Except, of course, that it didn't save him," pointed out Tania. "At least, from someone's actions. And you'll probably be pleased to hear that I've nearly finished explaining what those possible actions could have been prompted by. There's just one more person to consider, and that's the one who could potentially have been closer to Professor Kates than any of you. I mean, of course, Ivan Ocean, a student at Camford University, where the professor was such a prominent academic."

"But I've said," protested Ivan, "the professor and I hardly crossed paths at all. He was nothing to do with my course. I scarcely knew him. So why would I want to harm him?"

"Because," resumed Tania, "it seems that the professor had his fingers in many pies at the university, and one of those pies was the matter of the finances of the Students Union. Ivan, as we know, has a very responsible position at the Union. He is in charge of financial matters. But it appears that the professor, for some reason, had come to be interested in those finances. We can unfortunately only speculate as to why – perhaps another student official had gone to him with concerns. Perhaps a routine audit had thrown up questions. The only thing we can be certain of is that during last Saturday's function, Professor Kates dropped some very heavy hints that Ivan's financial conduct was up for investigation. He spoke about accounting – or to use his word, 'unaccountable' – discrepancies, and interesting revelations. If Ivan had indeed been dipping his fingers into the till, such revelations could be dangerous. At the least, they could result in his rustication – forgive the obscure language, but that's the term used for expulsion from the university - and a blight on any planned future career path. At worst, they could lead to charges of fraud, and if Ivan were to be found guilty, the serious prospect of prison. That is a danger that someone might wish to avoid at all costs. Was murder seen as the only way to eliminate that danger?"

"I don't understand, Tania," piped up Annette Curtin. "You've talked about all these other people, but you haven't mentioned me. Not that I mind, of course. Even the thought of killing somebody makes me shudder. But why are you so sure that I shouldn't be on your list? And what about the others? Those men who were running the murder evening? And then there's Alexandra here, and that nice-looking young man from the television – Lindsey, wasn't it? And where is he anyway?"

"For one thing, Lindsey is working away," explained Tania. "And for another thing, he, and Alex, and you, have all been ruled out because you never left the supper room during the crucial period during which the murder must have taken place. You had no opportunity to commit the crime, and opportunity is one of the three things which are usually considered in a case such as this. That, together with means and motive. The motives I've already covered. As for the means, it's almost certain that the antique truncheon was the weapon used."

Inspector Marion Bright interrupted Tania's flow. "You can omit the word 'almost' from that sentence, Mrs Faye," she said. "We've had conclusive results from our forensic people, and the truncheon is confirmed as the fatal item."

"Thank you for that, inspector," replied Tania.

"I'm grateful, although what you say doesn't affect my thinking. You see, all along I've been convinced that the truncheon was crucial. And its whereabouts even more so. Because it became clear that it had been removed from the evidence table in the art gallery, used in a swift and fatal attack on Professor Kates, and then just as swiftly replaced. But how and by whom? Some people were adamant that the truncheon was in place when they examined the clue items. Some said it was absent. They could not all be right. And so there was a persistent state of uncertainty. Until, that is, a second attack took place.

"My part-time assistant Jenny Chandler, who you will remember was working as your waitress at the function last Saturday, was intrigued by the mystery and determined to help in finding a solution. I may even bear a tiny amount of blame for that myself, in that I have been caught up in two murders previously, and have played some small part in solving them. And on Wednesday Jenny, after leaving her normal job at the surgery, came into the library with the intention of examining the scene of the crime to see if anything struck her. As, unfortunately, it did. She was looking around the special exhibition area when something incongruous caught her eye. Something yellow. But before she could look more closely, she was stabbed in the back. There are just two fortunate aspects. Firstly, that the blow was mis-delivered, and did not damage any vital organs. Secondly, that my husband Ron and I arrived on the scene, apparently only minutes later, and were able to call for help, so that Jenny is now recovering from what could have been a fatal injury. So no second murder, thank goodness."

"But why was there no witness?" queried Alex. "Didn't you see anybody? And what about the reception desk in the Town Hall foyer? The staff there must surely have seen somebody."

"Cuts," replied Ron shortly. "The council is saving money, so the reception desk is unstaffed after five o'clock. There is only a telephone there which callers can use to contact the switchboard. And telephones do not make very good eye witnesses."

"But can't you eliminate anyone?" said Alex. "Surely not everybody could have been in the Town Hall at that moment."

"I'm afraid you're wrong," said Tania. "Any one of the people I've spoken of could have been present. Most live or work in and around Ramston, and those who don't were free of the commitments which would have kept them away. But it is clear to me that there is only one person who could have been responsible for the attack, and therefore also responsible for the death of Professor Kates. And funnily enough, inspector, it was a remark of yours which finally put me on the right track."

Marion Bright looked at Tania in surprise. "But I really don't see how ..."

"Let me explain. On Wednesday evening, Jenny came through the pass door from the library to look around in here. I'd given her my key so that she could get in. And she caught sight of something which drew her attention. Now it had already been reasonably established that the fatal weapon was the police truncheon, but that was examined afterwards, and was shown to bear no fingerprints other than those of the game organisers. Therefore a glove had most probably been used. And when the list of the clue items laid out on the evidence table was enumerated by my husband, who it

230

seems has an exceptional visual memory, there was a discrepancy. Originally there had been a pair of yellow household gloves. Afterwards, there was only one. So the truncheon was held by the glove, used in the attack, and then replaced. But to replace the glove presented a danger to the perpetrator. We've probably all seen crime shows on television. It's well-known that traces of DNA within a glove will provide positive identification. So the glove had to be got out of the way. It couldn't be removed from the scene, since nobody had the opportunity to leave. It couldn't be retained on the murderer's person, because if discovered it would be a deadly giveaway. It had to be concealed, and the only place was somewhere in the art gallery. And that is why it was stuffed down behind a radiator in the hope of remaining unnoticed. As it did."

"And believe me," growled Inspector Bright, "I shall be having harsh words with the forensics department on that subject. Somebody may need to look to their job."

"But you still don't tell us who this mysterious person is," persisted Annette. "And what does some remark by the inspector have to do with it?"

"First, there was a comment by Professor Kates, overheard by you, Annette, and reported to me by Jenny when she came into the library on Tuesday evening. The words 'hand in glove' were used. Did the murderer hear them and fear that Jenny knew more than she actually did? It meant that the glove had to be recovered as soon as circumstances allowed. And the murderer set out for the deserted Town Hall foyer with that intention, now that it was known that the police had cleared the scene, except that now Jenny was in the way. She needed

231

to be removed before she discovered something incriminating. And so a knife was seized from the 'Kitchen Sink Drama' display and used on Jenny, who collapsed behind the display. The rubber glove was recovered from its hiding place. I imagine that it's probably been destroyed by now. Then what? Jenny still had the key to the pass door in her hand. The murderer quickly grabbed it and used it to lock the pass door from the gallery side in the hope of delaying discovery, and then fled the scene. But they forgot about one thing. The rubber glove had been used to avoid leaving fingerprints on the truncheon. But what about the tell-tale fingerprints left in haste on the pass key?"

"No, because I wiped ..." Monica de Glenn bit off the words she was about to speak and froze. There was a sudden silence.

"Because you wiped the key clean, were you about to say, Miss de Glenn?" enquired the inspector silkily.

"No ... what I mean is ... whoever did this ... must have ..." Monica's voice trailed away, and she visibly crumpled in her seat.

"The person who overheard those words 'hand in glove' from Jenny to me was you, Monica," stated Tania. "Nobody else knew about them, save Annette. So then we come back to the remark from you, Inspector, which triggered a train of thought in my brain. In the hospital, you warned Jenny and me about the dangers of setting ourselves up as some sort of detective. 'It creates a false impression', you said. And suddenly, that made sense of the comments which Professor Kates was heard to make to Monica while the two were standing in front of the painting by Alfred Sisley in the art gallery. A painting Kates didn't seem to

232

think much of. But was that because he didn't care much for the work of the impressionist school? Or was it because he had doubts about the authenticity of the painting? Its provenance was mysterious. He had apparently studied art in some depth in his own student days, so he would have been aware of nuances of style. And he commented on Monica's mastery of style. He described her as a very talented painter. But later he said something which one of you here heard, but which they didn't understand. 'Almost perfect' he said 'but almost isn't good enough'. And then a door closed, as the professor returned to the reading room. So what was Monica to do? Clearly the professor had identified a work which he believed Monica had produced – a forgery. If revealed, that would be the end of her career, and as a convicted fraudster, most probably her freedom. There must have been very little time to think. Monica had just enough forethought to put on the rubber glove to protect herself before grabbing the truncheon and following the professor into the reading room, with the result we are all too well aware of. Then, back to the table, replace the truncheon, conceal the glove, and attempt to act normally. But Monica later told a lie in order to divert attention away from herself. She said that the truncheon had already gone when she arrived at the evidence table. But Roland said that he believed it was probably still there, and he was examining the clue prior to Monica. Another tiny detail which I should have picked up sooner."

Monica heaved a profound sigh. "I don't know what I was thinking. I suppose I wanted to give the professor one last chance to relent. But he wouldn't even look at me. Just gave a snort of contempt as he looked at those damned notes in front of him. And I was frightened. I didn't want to. So I ..." She stood. "I don't suppose anything I say will make any difference. There's no point in bleating about an artist's hard life, when to tell the truth, I've always been comfortable. But I'd turned out so many copies of works of art for people at cheap prices that one day I thought, why not make a decent profit for myself for a change. I needed a substantial amount of money to set up my bronze forge. And impressionists are easy – or so I thought. I could do Sisley's style, so I invented a picture and then put it out there through an unscrupulous art dealer I knew. And that picture was purchased by the Ramston Art Gallery. Oh, the dealer got a cut." She turned to Bright. "If it will help me, Inspector, there are some details about the illicit trade I can give you." She sighed once more. "It's always the details, isn't it?"

"It is indeed, Miss de Glenn," said Marion Bright. "And I'm very grateful for your admission. Because you thought you had forgotten the detail about your fingerprints on the library pass door key. In fact, you hadn't. You had made a very good job of wiping the key clean, except for one tiny partial print which we may or may not be able to identify as yours. Just to go back to the professor's words, your job of wiping the key was almost perfect, but almost wasn't good enough. Sergeant Miner, if you would be so good ..."

The sergeant rounded the table and placed a hand on Monica's shoulder. "Monica de Glenn, I am arresting you for the murder of Professor Russell Kates, and for the attempted murder of Jennifer Chandler. You do not have to say anything ..."

As the sergeant continued through the formula,

and conducted Monica out of the reading room, all those remaining exchanged stunned looks.

"Well, that's that," said Ron into the silence, putting his arm around his wife's shoulders. "Now let's go home."

Epilogue

"You don't say," marvelled Dennis Dean, wide-eyed, as Tania and Ron enjoyed a leisurely drink, perched at the bar in the Cross Keys prior to Sunday lunch. "Who'd have thought it? Well, there's a turn-up for the books."

"And now," said Ron, "my dear wife is going to take a break from murder in all its forms. I'm not even going to let her read any Agatha Christie."

"I'm just going to go back to being an ordinary small-town librarian," agreed Tania with a smile.

"And I don't blame you," said Dennis. "So you two go and sit down, and I'll be bringing your lunches over in a couple of minutes. Although I admit," he added, "I shall miss the excitement."

"I've had quite enough excitement to last me a lifetime," laughed Tania. "No more mysterious deaths for me."

"Oh?" said Dennis, his eyes sparkling. "So you won't be interested in the story on the local radio this morning?"

"What story?" asked Tania warily.

"You know that dig they've been doing on the prehistoric barrow up on the Downs the other side of Westchester?" explained Dennis. "Well, so far they'd found five sets of human remains."

"And ...?"

"This morning they found another set. Except this time, it's the chief archaeologist." Dennis raised an eyebrow in Tania's direction.

"No!" declared Tania firmly. "No, no no!"

"Come on, love," said Ron, linking his arm with his wife's. "Let's have lunch." He looked back at Dennis with a wink and a murmured 'We'll see'.

*   *   *

also by Roger Keevil

The Inspector Constable Murder Mysteries

Murderer's Fête
Who could have foreseen the murder of a clairvoyant
at a country fête?

Murder Unearthed
Sun, sangria and suspects during a supposed holiday
in Spain

Death Sails In The Sunset
Murder ensues when a journalist won't let guilty
secrets be buried at sea

Murder Comes To Call
Three short stories to tax the talents of our detectives

Murder Most Frequent
Another trilogy of intriguing cases for Constable and
Copper

The Odds On Murder
Who is riding for a fall when a prominent racehorse
trainer is killed?

No Bar To Murder
Complicated relationships make a potent and lethal
cocktail

The Murder Cabinet
A return to Dammett Hall leaves the nation's fate in
the team's hands

The Game Of Murder
Sudden death at the TV studio as entertainment turns
to murder;
PLUS a bonus short story, 'Exit A Murderer',
and a full index to all the Inspector Constable
mysteries

The Copper & Co Murder Mysteries

Honeymooner's Murder
Even on an idyllic tropical island, murder never takes
a holiday

Murder At Witch's Holt
Dark secrets lead to a strange death at a spooky
manor house

Buccaneer's Murder
A wealthy businessman lies dead aboard his luxury
private yacht

The Ramston Murder Mysteries

Murdered By Moonlight
Dramatic death at a Cornish open-air theatre

Manuscript For Murder
An ancient abbey with an all-too-modern corpse

Printed in Great Britain
by Amazon